Until Death Does She Part

AMBER LEIGH LARRAIN

To my husband:
Our fights should be a masterclass in respectful discourse
We laugh endlessly
You are my forever cheerleader in everything I do
We've changed over the years but always grow in tandem

In other words, deciding to spend forever with you was the best impulsive decision I've made in a TGI Fridays

Also by Amber Leigh Larrain

Psychological Thrillers :

Blackout Girl

Everyone I Love Is Dead - March 2026

Cozy Fantasy:

Spellbound Beneath Sapphire Skies - Sept 2025

"The husband did it," - Everyone Obsessed With True Crime

Excerpt from the personal journal of Lyle Lazrin, Dated summer 2014

Shelley was like the opposite ends of the Earth. Bright, Warm and full of growth at one end, Dark, Cold and desolate at the other. But she kept on spinning, kept on going-because what else could she do?

And she was like my Earth- She was my home. And I was slowly killing her.

Chapter One

February 2025

LYLE TUCKED the chocolate cupcake mix, vanilla frosting and bottle of red wine under his arm and made a beeline for the check-out. He knew Shelley would be sitting at home tapping her watch impatiently. Each line was five people deep, all stocking up for what looked like a family of forty-five. He muttered a curse under his breath.

Then, at the end, the number fourteen light flickered on and he bolted for it. A woman wearing a black, cat-ear, headband, pushing a cart filled with single serve frozen dinners got there before him.

If Lyle was anything, he was extremely charming. His good looks and outgoing personality made him instantly likable. This was often used to his advantage. As the woman began to unload her cart, he said, "I like the cat ears. Very cute! Mind if I cut in front? I only have three things." He held them up, raising his eyebrows as both an ask and a plea.

The woman didn't look up but touched the fuzzy headband a bit self-consciously. She tilted her head to signal, 'Go ahead,' as she pulled back the frozen dinners to make room for his small purchase.

"Thanks," he said as he shuffled past her. "My wife's a real hard ass and told me I needed to be back in ten minutes. Apparently, it's a cupcake emergency." Lyle flashed his bright white smile.

The cashier laughed and smiled back. Her eyes lit up. "Hey, don't I know you?" asked the young woman as she scanned his items.

"You might! I've got the billboard on 195 and a few smaller signs around town. I'm a real estate agent. So, when you are ready to move out of your parents' house, look me up! I'll help you find something." Even on a quick trip to the grocery store, he still found a way to talk about work.

"Sure! Everything in this area is so expensive though. I can't even afford to rent a room at this point. I'll probably be at home for a long time," the cashier complained.

He sympathetically nodded. She wasn't wrong.

"That will be, $27.85."

Lyle tapped his card and said, "I understand. Well, I'll be around when you are ready. Have a good one!" He grabbed the goods and the receipt, then yelled a thanks over his shoulder to the woman who let him cut the line as he headed to the exit.

Lyle got into the car, with the required goods. He and Shelley had been arguing all morning over finances, chores and whatever else she could find to bicker over. He hoped this would get him back into her good graces.

As he drove the route back home, he passed the large billboard with his face on it. 'Lyle Lazrin, Beach Front Properties' was printed across the top in bold blue font, his face with a dazzling white smile beneath it. He noted that the corner was starting to peel off and he would have to call the billboard company to fix it.

Pulling into the driveway, he once again double-checked that he had everything on her list, just to be sure. When he entered the house, he found Shelley in the small home office. Despite not working for several years, she was often in this spot. Shelley was hunched over the keyboard and he could see by the look on her face, cupcakes and wine were not going to help.

Lyle approached cautiously. "Hey..." he said.

She looked up briefly and then back at her computer before responding. "Hey. Put the stuff in the kitchen. I have no time to make these damn cupcakes for the event tomorrow. I'm just... I'm just so overwhelmed."

He lightly put his hand on her shoulder. "I could make them. Can't guarantee that they will be edible but if it helps you out, I'm willing to try."

She laughed and he saw her relax a bit as she mentally checked off one item on her never-ending to-do list. "Well, the PTA just asked for cupcakes, they didn't say they needed to be good. I appreciate it."

As Lyle walked around the kitchen, he frequently checked back to the list on the box. Trying to find all the necessary items to make cupcakes was like going on a treasure hunt. He was completely out of his element. While he shared equal cooking duties with his wife and enjoyed being in the kitchen, he couldn't bake to save his life. Steak and mashed potatoes were more his specialty.

It was worth it, he thought. The old mantra 'Happy wife, Happy Life' popped into his head as he cracked the egg over the large blue bowl. There had been so much conflict over the past few weeks, arguments he couldn't even exactly recall, and it was wearing him down.

As he poured the remaining ingredients into the bowl, Shelley walked up behind him. She placed a hand on his shoulder. Not exactly the intimacy he hoped for, but it was a start.

She kissed his cheek. "Thanks again."

He looked over at her and was trying to judge by her facial expression if she was in a joking mood or not. What the hell, he thought and went for the innuendo, "You could thank me in other ways, you know." He lifted his eyebrows up and down while running his hand down her back.

She laughed, but not in the way he hoped. More like ridicule.

"You look cheesy when you do that. And yeah, I don't even know if I have time to shower today...let alone *that.*"

The way she emphasized 'that' really made him want to toss one of these lousy cupcakes at her. "It's been a month. God, forbid you make time for *that.*"

"Well, I'm sorry if I'm exhausted."

His wife began a familiar rant and he zoned it all out, stewing over her rejection. He waited until she fell silent. "Sorry to hear that," he said flatly, turning his attention back to the cupcakes.

Shelley rolled her eyes. "You weren't even listening."

"I was," Lyle responded defensively. And even though he hadn't been, she complained about the same things over and over so he could just regurgitate it. "The PTA is too much work, for no pay. God forbid anyone said thank you! Kerri on the PTA is a PITA. You're doing more than a 9-5 job but aren't paid a dime, and no one notices. You haven't had a good night's sleep since 2011. You are tired all the time. And Kylie's activities have made you into a goddamn chauffeur." He gave her a self-satisfied smile.

"Okay, okay, I was wrong," she admitted, tossing her hands in the air. She walked back to the computer without another word.

He had no idea what she was even working on.

Shelley was in the bathroom, door ajar, getting ready to take their twelve-year-old daughter Kylie out. She had put on her new purple 'Belmar Blaze Basketball' sweatshirt and a new pair of jeans. The older ones were too snug, just another thing making her feel restricted. Her closet was full of shoes she had never worn before and to be honest couldn't recall when she even bought them. A pair of dark purple sneakers went well with the sweatshirt and she slipped her feet into them for the first time.

The mother daughter duo had planned to try a new Mexican restaurant in Asbury Park. Ever since Kylie, her only daughter, had become a tween, things had been rocky. She hoped tonight would go smoothly.

Kylie called out, "What time are we leaving?"

"Is fifteen minutes good? I'd like to do my hair and makeup," she called back.

"Yeah, fine."

Shelley continued to get ready. As she took out her makeup bag, she thought how she was looking forward to some quality time with her daughter and a good meal. After applying some foundation and mascara, she tried to use her new curling iron to get the 'beach wave' look. Unfortunately, it just looked like tight ringlets. Gazing at her reflection, she laughed because her hair looked more 'Shirley Temple' than the look she was going for. Oh well, she still liked it, she thought.

She walked into Kylie's room and let her know she was ready.

Kylie swiveled around in her chair. "You spent all that time and that's what you look like?"

Shelley stood there shocked. Sure, Kylie often gave her attitude but nothing like this before. She never would have talked to her mother like that. "That was really...unnecessary..." she responded, her voice cracking. She wasn't exactly sure when things became so tense between them. Long gone were the toddler days where Kylie followed her around everywhere smiling and laughing. The conflict only added to the ever-growing pressures of her life.

"You're supposed to brush it out after, so it doesn't look like... that," Kylie said.

Shelley turned around without response, walked out of her room and out the front door. Kylie sometimes got into this mood—like she wanted to tear the entire world down. For Kylie, she was just trying to push boundaries, stir the pot. For Shelley, words that cut her down always sucked the life out of her and left her feeling empty.

. . .

Lyle, seeing his wife walk out alone, door slamming behind her, walked into Kylie's room to investigate. "What just happened? Where did mom go?"

Kylie shrugged.

He narrowed his eyes. "Tell me what happened," he said more forcefully.

"Eh, I said something she didn't like."

He walked up to his daughter. "Something she didn't like or something rude?" When she didn't respond he answered his own question. "So, something rude. Why would you do that?" he said, taking her phone. "You are done for the night. I doubt she's going to take you out and you've lost your phone. It literally takes zero effort to be kind—especially to someone who does so much for you."

Lyle turned to leave the room as Kylie called, "How long did I lose it for?"

Lyle didn't even look back. "That's the least of your concerns."

Kylie got up to follow him out of the room and started to protest, a night without her phone seemed a pretty extreme punishment in her eyes. "That's so unfair! I barely said anything. What am I supposed to do all night?"

"God, forbid you do something off of a screen for a few hours. Read a book, go for a walk."

"Dad! Please," she begged.

"Nope, maybe spend the time thinking about how you treat people and how it makes them feel."

She rolled her eyes and crossed her arms mumbling again about how unfair it was.

Lyle tried to call Shelley but she didn't answer. He checked her location and she was strolling along the nearby beach. That would be good for her, he thought and he left her to her thoughts, allowing her some space to deal with her emotions.

It was another two hours before she returned home, her face streaked with tears. When she walked in, he embraced her and she melted into him.

"I just don't get how you can give birth to something, give it everything it needs to thrive and then it can be such a little sh-shrimp dumpling."

"Yeah, she is definitely being a little sh-shrimp dumpling right now," Lyle responded and she laughed. It was good to see her smile.

"It's just a phase you know. She's just got a lot of changes in her life right now with middle school and growing up. It's not about you. She's just figuring herself out."

Shelley agreed. "But I just wish it didn't hurt so much."

"I know, but we love you Shels." He kissed her on the head and she wrapped her arms around him tighter.

"How was your walk?"

"I mean, I was crying for most of it. And it was pretty cold and windy! So not great. But I had this strange feeling while I was out there."

"Like what?"

"Like someone was following me. I don't know—that sounds crazy right?"

"They were probably just strolling along like you were. I mean, the beach only goes in two directions. I wouldn't worry about it."

"Yeah," she said.

But he could see by her facial expression that she felt ill at ease. "You have to stop listening to so much true crime. It's getting in your head. We live in a safe town! Nothing to worry about. Maybe swap out the true crime for audiobooks."

Shelley laughed but nodded in agreement. "That's a good idea."

"Are you hungry? There is some pasta on the stove. Sorry—it's not much. I thought I'd be the only one home for dinner tonight. I'm going to do some work in the office," he said, giving her a quick kiss on the cheek. "You'll be okay?"

She nodded, went to the kitchen alone, scooped some dinner into a bowl and ate, the ginger cat at her feet, her only companion.

Chapter Two

LYLE WALKED into the bar and searched around. In the back corner he saw two of his friends and headed towards them.

Xavier got up and slapped him on the back. "Hey! You made it."

Lyle smiled as they both slide back into the booth. He couldn't make it last week because Shelley was having a difficult night after Kylie's unkind words. She told him he could go but he felt like she needed him to stay with her. He hadn't told them that of course. What lie had he told them? He had forgotten already.

The waitress took his order—a beer, wings, and fries.

His other friend Mason asked, "How was the practice?"

Right, he had told them he needed to help out with Kylie's basketball practice. They didn't have kids yet, so they didn't know that was an unlikely scenario—they had paid coaches on the team. Not to mention, he didn't have the skill set to coach the sport. "It was good. I was just an extra set of hands. She has a really great coach this year."

Mason took a large swig of his beer.

"How's Becca?" Lyle asked.

Mason chatted away about Becca, who was expecting their first child in three months. Lyle nodded his head but he was thinking about Shelley. What if she completely shut down and needed him now? What if her mind went into overdrive while he was away and wasn't there to help her? He thought about the times that happened and how sometimes a week later they'd end up with fifteen packages on their doorstep…or how she once stayed up for twenty-four hours writing a fantasy novella, hated and deleted it all.

"Lyle!" Mason shouted.

Lyle laughed awkwardly. "Sorry. It's loud in here and I'm having a hard time hearing you. Guess I'm getting old! What did you say?"

"I asked how Shelley was doing?"

He felt resentful that even when he had the time to go out with friends, Shelley's issue, whatever the hell was happening with her, were invading his thoughts. He just wanted one night to be able to relax and have a good time with his friends. "Yeah…good. Still looking for work. She's keeping busy with the PTA and Kylie's activities. Overall, she's doing great," he lied.

Why couldn't he just talk to his friends about this stuff? Isn't that what friends were for? But he felt this overwhelming pressure to maintain a level of success. He constantly had to keep up this image of marital and fatherly perfection. That's why he had secretly started getting Botox and teeth whitening for the past two years. Ever since his fortieth birthday, he had been trying to hide the signs of aging.

In the back of his mind, he felt like everything else would fall apart if he didn't portray this image. So here he was spending week after week with friends, painting for them a picture of a life that didn't really exist. He might as well have been reading them a fairy tale.

The waitress brought Lyle's food and he stayed with his friends for a few hours. As the night wore on, his frustration at himself, or them—he didn't know—grew. His mind wandered as they talked. It felt pointless to be there when everything felt so fake. For the rest of the night, Lyle focused on eating and mostly pretending to listen. His friends didn't seem to notice his sudden withdrawal.

· · ·

When Lyle awoke the next morning, he found Shelley staring out of the large bay window that overlooked the road. He wanted to say something cheesy like 'Penny for your thoughts.' But by the time he could think of something less ridiculous to say, she had turned around to face him.

"Do you ever think there is something more within you? Like there are limitless possibilities. That there are beautiful words swirling in your head, waiting to be written, if you could just organize your thoughts and get a few hours of quiet. But the time never becomes available and the words never get a chance to come together, so they just swirl endlessly, the limitless possibilities, floating just out of reach?" Her dark brown eyes looked at him, almost begging, to be understood.

"No," he replied quietly. Her thoughtful words falling flat on him. He had everything he wanted. And she had everything she needed, but nothing she wanted.

"Okay," she said with a weak smile.

The two-word exchange held so much more. A disconnect. A marriage that was somehow wonderful and a profound disappointment all at once.

* * *

Excerpt from the personal diary of Shelley Lazrin, Dated Aug 2010

Today was my wedding day. The day most girls dream of their entire life. I'm happy- but am I as happy as I should be? How do we ever know if this is the happiest we will ever be- or if there is something greater out there that we just don't get to experience because we stopped looking?

Does Lyle deserve someone who is over the moon at this moment? And when will all these questions stop obsessively swirling around in my head? I just want some quiet.

I wanted to be a writer. Before that, I wanted to be an interior decorator. I can't even recall what it was before that. But today- I'm just a wife. Just a wife.

I've heard "behind every great man is a great woman." What the hell does that mean for me? That my dreams are on hold to support his? I don't know. Maybe someday I'll write, or decorate houses, or travel the world and post pictures that make everyone think "Wow, her life is so glam" or I'll remember the vanished dreams and I'll take hold of those...or maybe they will remain forgotten so I can be a good wife.

We had a party after the wedding reception, for those who weren't ready to go home. Lyle got way too drunk. I didn't care- it was kinda funny. Tessa claimed he was flirting with her sister, but it didn't even piss me off. Tessa on the other hand was livid. I told her that's just how Lyle is, he's charming, a talker. After enough of her going on and on about it, I walked up to him and said we'd better go. And you know what torrid thing they were talking about? Real estate! I had to laugh. Tessa can be too much sometimes. Lyle was trying to tell her about how he thinks getting into real estate, especially by the shore, is where the money is.

We left hand in hand, unsure of the road ahead. Excited, hesitant, nervous.

So that is how our life together begins.

Chapter Three

LYLE SAT in their shared home office. Shelley had decorated it in a nautical theme that weaved throughout the house. The walls were the color of the sea on a dark night. A large painting of a yacht on the water hung above him.

The phone rang and he quickly picked it up. "Lyle Lazrin of Beach Front Properties. How can I help you find your next dream home with the ocean as your backyard?"

From the living room, Shelley could hear the conversation. She cringed a little every time he answered the phone like that. He sounded more like a used car salesman to her than a high-end real-tor. Lyle had been selling houses along the Jersey shore for a decade now and she had to admit he was damn good at it.

They had started their life together in a suburb outside of Philly where she grew up. Their house was small and run-down. After he got his footing in real estate, they were able to afford moving to Belmar themselves. While their house wasn't as large as the houses he sold and it was a few blocks walk to the water, she adored it. She had spent years turning it into the perfect coastal chic escape. It was like being on vacation all the time.

Shelley truly loved this town. It was quiet for most of the year. A real small, tight knit community.

From Memorial Day to Labor Day, it morphed into a bustling town with new people each week, eager to spend the day laying around on the sandy beach. She enjoyed this dichotomy. At this point, she couldn't imagine living anywhere else.

"Tell me a little about what you are looking for? Okay...Okay... Sure, I have at least three places in mind that fit that description. When do you want to meet? Yes...that sounds good. I'll text you the location for the first address, see you soon." He put his phone on the desk and rubbed his hands together.

"Another client?"

Lyle smirked. "What can I say? They want to meet tomorrow morning. Can you take Kylie to school? I want to get there early."

Shelley agreed.

The next morning, Lyle got himself ready before anyone in the house was awake. He slicked back his thick black hair and put on dress pants, a button-down shirt, and a tie with a beach scene on it—this was his go to work outfit.

He drove out to the agreed upon meeting place and was there fifteen minutes early. He hoped to look around first, just to verify they still had the house nicely staged. Lyle unlocked the door and called inside to make sure no one was home, though he was pretty sure that the elderly couple had done as most New Jerseyans did when they turned eighty—sold their home and moved to Florida.

This house hadn't been on the market long but already had many showings. Due to the high traffic, he noticed some footprints on the upstairs landing and took out some wet wipes to clean it up. He went around and made sure everything looked meticulous. Lyle was pretty confident he could leverage the amount of showings to ramp up the client's interest in this home.

As he peeked into the last room, a small guest room with peach walls and a day bed, he heard something downstairs. It sounded like the door shutting and then shuffling of papers. "Hello? Is someone there?" It just occurred to him that he hadn't even gotten the name of the client he was meeting.

Lyle walked down the steps to greet them, but no one was there. He tried to open the door to see if they were on the porch but the deadbolt had been locked. "What the hell?" he said aloud, knowing it was only possible to lock it from the inside. If someone else came in and locked the deadbolt, they were still in the house with him. "Hello?" he called out, trying to tamper down any fear in his voice.

Then Lyle wrote the whole thing off—he must have locked the door himself and forgotten. The client must have developed cold feet, probably realizing this home was out of their budget. It was frustrating but it was just a fact of life in this industry.

Lyle walked from room to room, looking in every nook and cranny of the house. Nothing was out of place. His client was now running fifteen minutes late. He tried calling the number they provided, and an automated voice informed him that the number was no longer in service.

His phone rang as he was locking up the home, and he quickly fumbled to answer it, hoping it was the client. "Hmmm hmmm... hmmmm hmmm. Fantastic news." A huge smile spread across Lyle's face. *When one door shuts, another one opens*, he said to himself. "Yes, tomorrow at 10:30 is perfect. I'll meet you at the office with all the paperwork. Thanks again!" With a closing on the horizon, he pushed the time wasted this morning out of his mind. He was about to close one of the biggest sales of his career.

"You won't believe this!" Shelley exclaimed as she walked through the door.

"I have a feeling I will," Lyle responded, deadpan.

She playfully hit his shoulder. "Kerri took a bite off one of the cupcakes, even though they were supposed to be for the bake sale but whatever. So, Kerri nearly chokes on the cupcake—"

"That's a good thing, right?" Lyle joked.

Shelley let out a small snort and tried to hide her smile. She continued her story without comment. "So, she's making a big deal about how dry they are, for what purpose? Just to take a dig at me! Liza quietly told her to hush. So, Tessa is getting herself all worked up and takes another cupcake, like will any of these cupcakes actually go to the kids?! Anyway, she's trying so hard to act like these cupcakes are good, to prove Kerri wrong, but it's true—you made awful cupcakes." Shelley was about to erupt into a fit of giggles.

"Maybe that was my secret plan all along so I didn't have to bake again."

She let out a little laugh. "Good plan! So, she popped the whole thing into her mouth and it's like she had a wad of peanut butter in there. She couldn't talk for five minutes."

"Riveting story, Sweetie! I'm going to pitch this as a reality show —The Real PTA Moms of Belmar."

Shelley couldn't hold it back anymore and she burst out laughing, falling into him. No matter what was going on in their lives, they could always make each other laugh.

He kissed her forehead and then she glanced up at him. "You know, I don't care if you haven't showered," he said, pushing his luck.

She made a face like she was considering it. "Maybe another time." And she looked up at him, giving him a quick peck on the lips.

"So, my client didn't show up today...total waste of time. But it wasn't a total waste of the day. Some other things panned out."

"Good news?"

"Maybe...but never mind that. So...you know how you wanted to visit Hawaii?"

"Oh my god! Don't tell me!"

"Okay, I won't." And he turned to walk away.

"Lyle, get your tuchas back here! Did you close on the McMansion in Spring Lake?!"

"I told you to stop calling them that. They are luxury beach front homes for the modern family," he said in a playful, fancy voice. "But...I sure did!" And she leapt into his embrace as he wrapped his arms around her, taking in the smell of her vanilla perfume. They loved to travel and closing on one of the larger beach houses always gave them a pretty good windfall to go someplace exciting.

The next day, Lyle headed home right after closing on the house, a chilled bottle of champagne in his hand. He was ready to celebrate.

"Shelley?" he called out. He knew she was home because her red convertible, which she had impulsively bought three years ago without consulting him, was in the driveway. There was no response. He walked through the small house calling her name and was met with silence. When he got to their bedroom, he could hear her sniffling in the adjoining bathroom.

He gently tapped on the door. "Shel, I know you are in there, can I come in?" Again, no response. "I'm opening the door, so if you don't want me to come in, say so now." He slowly opened the bathroom door, and there she was, laying on the ground in a heap, hot tears streaking her face.

"What's wrong?" he asked gently. He never knew how she would respond in these moments. As she continued to sob, he lowered himself onto the cold tile. He wished she could do these things on the warm carpet. He wished for a lot of things to be different actually. He placed his hand on her back, feeling her shaking. "Do you want to talk?"

She shook her head, unable to articulate what she needed in that moment. After sitting with her for close to twenty minutes, she spoke. "It's the anniversary."

"Shelley..." he started slowly. "Our anniversary is in August."

"Not *that* anniversary Lyle," she said with so much scorn, like his name was a curse word.

It clicked what she meant—he just never thought of it the same way she did. Three years ago, Shelley had lost a pregnancy at seven weeks. She hadn't even told him she was pregnant before she lost the baby. He found it incredibly sad but he moved on after some time and she never had.

"You don't care, do you? Lyle! This was our baby and you don't give a damn!" Her sadness had morphed to rage and transformed him too.

"God damnit, Shelley," he said, standing up. "We have to move on."

"Move on! Move on?!" she screamed at the top of her lungs.

He was thankful Kylie wasn't home to hear her. Shelley's rage was palpable and it seemed as if it shook everything around him. Unable to handle the emotions, he left the small bathroom and she followed him out.

"I'm not doing this with you now. I'm going to the gym."

"I swear to God, Lyle..." she said, inches from his face.

He could feel her hot breath and he took a step back to create some space. "What, Shelley? What will you do?"

With that she withered, crumbling to the ground again. When she got in this state, they were like the tides, simultaneously ebbing and flowing between emotions. Caring, sadness, anger, caring, sadness, anger.

"I just can't...cope," she cried.

He sat next to her again, too many emotions bubbling inside him. "You just really need to talk to someone."

"I'm trying to talk to you, Lyle," she cried.

"That's not what I mean and you know it."

"It didn't help," she said, almost childlike.

"It can if you let it. That was over a year ago and you only went a few times." He was too exhausted to argue about this with her. He let silence fill the air.

. . .

She balled up her fists and sucked in her lower lip. Shelley bit down hard, just so she could feel anything besides this emotional heartbreak. Her eyes closed and she could imagine the little three-year-old running around the bedroom, calling her name loudly. It hurt so badly that she ached to leave her body, this wretched body that couldn't keep her baby growing. "You think talking to someone, some stranger, is going to help me get over the fact that I should have my child here with me today? You think that I can just describe how I'm hurting. Lyle, words haven't even been created to describe my pain. And then what? Magically I'll stop thinking of how old they would be, what they would be doing right now. You think a god damn therapist, sitting there staring at me, is going to make me not watch my whole fucking life go by, imaging this child, OUR child, walking beside me?"

Lyle released a long and slow breath. He placed his hand on her back. He felt helpless and confused. *If only*, he thought, *I could snap my fingers and make everything better.*

The two sat in silence for a long while, only the sound of light sniffling interrupting the void of sound, a reminder that the hurt was still there even when nothing else was.

"You can go to the gym now," she said, her voice steady and he knew the storm had passed.

"No, it's fine. I want to be here with you," Lyle responded, knowing she was in too delicate a place right now to leave her alone. Lyle knew anything was possible when she was left alone in this state. It's why they had that damn expensive car they definitely shouldn't have gotten. It's why sometimes she would wander off without telling them where she was or when she'd be back. She laid her head on his shoulder and he let her, though he didn't return the affection.

. . .

Several nights later, a cold breeze swept through the room. Lyle turned over in bed and realized Shelley wasn't there. He waited a few minutes, thinking she might have gone to the bathroom or got a drink of water. He nodded off for a few minutes and when he came to, she still wasn't there. Lyle lugged himself out of bed and flicked on the light. He walked out into the living room and there was Shelley, hyper focused on whatever was on her laptop. She didn't look up as he approached.

"You okay?"

"Yes, yeah, I just couldn't sleep and so I planned out our trip." Lyle raised his eyebrows and then waited for her to explain. "I booked the flights and the hotel."

He nodded. "That probably didn't take you too long. It's 4 o'clock in the morning."

She patted the couch and he sat beside her, rubbing his eyes. Shelley clicked on a tab that showed an hour-by-hour agenda for a two-week vacation. He didn't know if he should feel worried or be impressed. In fact, he never knew how to react during her highs and lows. "How about you come to bed now?" he asked gently. The need for sleep was pulling at every muscle of his body like an anchor at sea.

"I'd rather go over this with you now and see what you think."

"Shel, it's 4am," Lyle said softly.

"Yes, you've just told me that," she replied, annoyed.

"So, I'd like to go to bed and I think it would be a good idea for you too."

Shelley sucked in a big breath as if this was a great sacrifice she was making.

"Will you join me? Please? I can rub your back to help you fall asleep if you need." He put his hand on her shoulder, hoping the connection might pull her from her work.

"No, sorry, I need to add in the address and phone number for each activity."

Lyle gave an almost imperceptible nod and kissed her gently on the head. He shut the bedroom window and went back into the icy bed. He tossed and turned for a while, worried about her, before drifting off to sleep.

Early next morning, Lyle heard Shelley typing in the small office. He walked in and greeted her warmly. "I was just outside and it's actually pretty warm for this time of year. Would you like to go for a quick walk? We should take advantage of it."

She kept typing. "No, I have a lot to do. Sorry."

He put his hand on her shoulder. "Shel, how long have you been working on that?"

She flipped her wrist and her watch turned on. "Wow! Okay, it's been nearly five hours."

"So why don't you take a little break and we can just enjoy the sunrise?"

She turned to face her husband. "Yes, you're right. I need a break from this screen," she said as she blinked her eyes rapidly.

Once they had put on their coats, they walked toward the boardwalk. She reached for his hand. He gave her a genuine smile. The sun over the ocean had streaked the sky a vibrant pink, splashed with clouds.

"Thanks, sometimes I don't realize when I need to step away."

He laughed. "I've known that about you for a while."

She playfully hit his arm and they sunk onto the cold sand. She scooped up a handful, and they watched as it slowly slipped through her fingers.

They looked straight ahead, watching the thick fluffy clouds saunter across the sky. At one point a cloud covered their view of the sun. It was like it had been swallowed up and the whole sky lost its luster.

Shelley twirled the wedding ring on her finger.

He took notice of her nervousness right away and instead of asking her about it, he wrapped his arm around her. "I'm sorry things have been a bit tense lately." He pulled her into him and she let her head fall onto the crook of his neck. He laid his head on top of hers, connected as if they were puzzle pieces made for each other. As the sun set further, the cold started to set in and the warmth they provided each other was welcomed.

"Is something wrong with me?" Shelley asked so quietly.

Lyle didn't even know what to say, but he knew he didn't want her hurting. "You're perfect," he said.

She laughed.

"What? You are!"

"Lyle, I'm a complete mess and I have no idea what's happening." She could always call him out on his bullshit.

"I understand that things aren't perfect right now—but that doesn't mean *you* aren't perfect. You need to see in yourself what the world sees in you."

Shelley raised her eyebrows doubtfully.

He took her chin in his hand and angled it so they were eye to eye. "What makes someone's life worth anything? It's the connections they make. It's the impact they have on those around them. You are by all accounts giving it your all to everyone and everything. See in yourself what every other damn person around you sees. A queen, a rockstar, a boss—I don't know what you want to call it but you are it, Shelley. You are it."

She continued to meet his gaze, taken aback by his words. She thought for a moment. "But would you say that about how I treat you too?"

Lyle looked back at the ocean. He watched the waves go in and out, in and out, like their relationship. "We have good days and ones that could be better, right?"

She agreed. "No matter what happens, you know I love you," she said.

"No matter what happens? Come on. You know we are together forever. Until death do they part." He reached for her hand.

"Until death does she part," she quipped.

He whipped his head to face her. "What the hell does that even mean?"

Her smile fell. "Sorry, I was trying to make a light-hearted joke about how crazy things have been for me lately. It was a stupid comment." She took her arm and looped it into his and then brought him closer.

"Don't joke about stuff like that. Look at me." He put his hand on her cheek and brought her to face him so they were eye to eye. "I'm serious."

"I was just kidding." Her voice was tinted with defensiveness.

"Yeah—but I'm not sure how else to say this—sometimes you put a lot of unnecessary stress on things."

She felt a bit embarrassed. "I don't mean to," she said, barely audible over the sound of waves crashing. "Do you ever feel like you are every emotion all at once? Like you want to be everything for everyone, and then it gets to be too much so you just want to run and hide and be nothing...to no one?"

He shrugged. He honestly couldn't relate.

Then, in a misguided effort to guide the conversation away, she ran her hand down his leg and whispered in his ear, "Want to do something to violate beach regulations?"

Lyle felt uncomfortable with the change in topic and laughed awkwardly. "You sure have a way with words today."

Though he knew this was an absolutely awful transition, it had been so long since she had even initiated intimacy and over a month since they'd been together. So, he kissed her deeply, combing his hands through her silky hair. They scurried beneath the boardwalk and then leaned back onto the sand. Lyle slowly moved his hand up her back, causing the cold sand to scratch her skin. The sound of a running group passing by on the above boardwalk made them both feel too vulnerable. The synchronous feet hitting the boards above loudly echoed in their ears.

They both started to laugh. "It's too cold for this, isn't it?"

Shelley nodded. "Too cold and too sandy," she said shaking the sand out of her hair.

"We wouldn't want to make those runners accomplices in our crime."

She kissed him quickly and then he got up, offering her his hand.

"That would be a pretty pathetic thing to get arrested for," she said.

"I don't know. Might make for a good story," he replied.

"Well, how about we use whatever we saved from the citation and put it towards a nice dinner out," she suggested jokingly.

"I'd like that. Let's move this to a more traditional setting."

They walked back to the house, hand in hand, making jokes about the situation the whole walk back. Once in the house, they entered the bedroom together, locking the door behind them.

Excerpt from the personal journal of Lyle Lazrin, Summer 2013

Shelley and I have been together now for three years- but something is different now. Most times things are normal. But some days are so dark. She won't get out of bed, she's hard on herself. It's painful to see her like that. But some days she's like a wind-up toy on overdrive...that's the only way I can explain it. Kylie is five months old and she decided she wanted to make a blanket for her. She taught herself to knit and stayed up for days- literal days- working around the clock on this blanket so she could finish it before she outgrows the bassinet... that's not normal right? I don't know...

* * *

Excerpt from the personal diary of Shelley Lazrin, Summer 2013

I've been off lately. Lyle asked me to talk to someone. I'm not against it but I just don't know if it's worth the time, especially with a baby. So, what if sometimes I can't sleep- I'm not the first person to have insomnia. And sometimes I can't get out of bed but I have an infant, I'm just tired... I don't seem to see it as this big problem like he does. It would be nice if he just accepted me for all that I am- highs and lows and the in between.

Chapter Four

Two weeks later, March 2025

SHELLEY LAID on the couch in beige oversized sweats, thankful for a moment of quiet and rest. Their large ginger cat, Gus Gus, cuddled on her lap, providing her extra warmth. A recently purchased travel book lay on the coffee table. She had read it all in one night and now it was just there as a reminder of something to look forward to. If all went to plan, later this summer they would all be laying on the beach.

Kylie was at basketball practice so she'd have forty-five minutes to herself before having to head back out to pick her up. Her mind buzzed with all the things she needed to do—look up recipes for next week, send out the PTA email, and fold the laundry. Those were all the big things. There were countless little things she also had on her to do list. They tore at her, a constant reminder that 'you aren't done, there is still so much to do.' It was both mentally and physically exhausting.

Ten minutes of contemplating how to use her time. Now she was down to just thirty-five. This is how it always went she thought. She picked up her cell phone and called her best friend Tessa.

Her friend picked up immediately and her overjoyed "HELLLLO," came through the speaker.

How does she do it? Shelley thought. *How does she manage life and not feel bogged down by all the pressure? Must be drugs*, she thought.

"Hey Tessa. How's it going?" Shelley pulled the phone away from her ear as Tessa's voice boomed from the speaker recounting the latest gossip. "So, what is it—Uppers? Cocktails? Seriously, how do you have this much energy? And you've got two more kids than I do!"

Tessa had been Shelley's friend since fifth grade and they grew closer when they both had daughters at the same time. Tessa was fun to be around, her over the top antics amusing to Shelley. For whatever issues people had with her, Shelley appreciated that she was always a straight shooter.

"Shelley, you don't have to do everything at 110%, things don't need to be perfect. Just...go with the flow and whatever happens, happens!"

Shelley smiled. "So, your sage life advice is to not give a fuck?"

Tessa's hearty laugh came through the speaker and Shelley couldn't help but laugh too. "Exactly."

After they hung up, she had about thirty minutes kid-free time and decided she'd see what her husband thought of this new approach.

She quietly opened the door and found him lying in bed with his phone, laughing. "What's funny?" she said trying to be light-hearted, but their recent past made it hard for him to interpret it that way.

"Come on. I'm allowed to come in here and relax, right? Or is there something I'm supposed to be doing?"

She rolled her eyes, thinking yes, actually, the dishes need to get done. Her carefree attitude had lasted twenty-four seconds, and most of that was walking from the couch to the bedroom. She was about to serve him up the same attitude he had given her, but her phone buzzed in her pocket and she froze for a second.

Shelley turned and walked in the hallway.

He called after her, "You know you don't have to leave the room every time you get a call!" And then he turned back to his phone, annoyed with the whole interaction.

"Hello?...Oh no! Okay, yeah. Yeah." Shelley quickly popped back into the room looking for her keys and purse. "Tell her I'm on my way. I'll be there in ten minutes."

Her husband looked at her with concern and she softened just a bit.

"That was Kylie's basketball couch, or the assistant rather. She isn't feeling well. I'm going to get her. Can you make some chicken noodle soup? For me too. I haven't been feeling well either. Must be something going around."

Lyle got up and agreed. He emptied a can of soup into a small pot and then started to play a game on his phone, completely losing track of time.

The liquid started boiling over when his phone chimed. He pulled it out and saw the time, 7:15. Kylie's practice ended at 7pm.

"Dad! Why hasn't anyone picked me up yet?"

"Mom came to pick you up early." He heard her huff on the other end of the line.

"Well obviously she didn't."

Lyle stood there for a moment, confused.

"Hello? Dad! Are you coming to get me? Or are you just going to leave me here all night?" The antics of a pre-teen were exhausting.

"I'll be right there."

And she hung up without saying goodbye.

Lyle put the phone into his pocket and headed to his daughter's middle school, scanning each street as he did so. Maybe Shelley's car broke down. That was the only logical explanation. Except, she would have called. She always had a charger in her car so the phone didn't die. Each turn he took without her red car coming into view, made his anxiety tick up a little more. Shelley wouldn't skip picking up their daughter, especially when she was sick. Part of his brain told him something was seriously wrong. The other part was trying to convince himself that there had to be some explanation for all of this. Something silly, like she accidentally went to her elementary school instead, and they would laugh about it later.

Kylie climbed into the Jeep with a scowl. "Thanks a lot. That was so embarrassing. I had to wait there alone with the coach for like twenty minutes. What am I supposed to talk to a forty-five-year-old about?"

Lyle let out a deep sigh—worry for his wife and exasperation for his pre-teen's angst swirled together. "I'm sorry you aren't feeling well. I made you soup."

Kylie scrunched up her face, the one that said, "Ugh, you are so weird."

"What?" he asked, confused.

"Dad, I'm fine."

"Your coach didn't seem to think so. Mom was told to come get you early."

"Yeah, clearly that didn't happen."

Lyle pulled the car to the shoulder. He scanned his daughter's face, trying to assess the situation. Then he recalled what Shelley had said and corrected himself. "Right, mom said it was the assistant coach."

"Dad! There is no assistant coach. It's just coach Myers. That's it. Maybe if you came to practice more, you'd know that. What is going on...?"

He hesitated—he didn't know how to respond. "I don't know. Mom's probably home now. It's just a mix up. No big deal, kiddo." He pulled back onto the road. He was portraying confidence in his words but his hand slipped on the wheel as they became damp with sweat. If he didn't see his wife's car in the driveway, he had no idea what to say or do.

Kylie stared at her phone and was oblivious to her father's rising anxiety. As he turned the corner his eyes darted back and forth looking for his wife's red convertible. No sign of it. He quickly dashed inside and went to their room, locking the door behind him.

He opened his phone and rang his wife. No answer. He called on repeat several times while peeking out the window, scanning the street for any sign of her. No answer, no sign of her. Each moment he felt his body creeping into panic mode. His hands trembled, making it difficult to use the touch screen. His mind was racing—a deluge of things he needed to do in that moment.

He called Tessa, trying to steady his voice.

She hadn't heard from her.

Her parents, Tom and Linda, hadn't heard from her. When his mother-in-law expressed concern he flipped the narrative—"Linda I'm so sorry! I got my days mixed up. She's probably still at the middle school for an event. Sorry to worry you." He hung up, ashamed of his lie. Where the hell was his wife?

Lyle walked into his daughter's room. She was at her desk, starting her math homework. "Hey sweetie. Can you take a break from that for a second?"

"I kinda need to do this now!" She swiveled around in her chair. "Dad...are you okay? You look like the one who is sick."

Lyle could feel the color drain from his face and his forehead was sweaty. "Yeah. About that call mom got to pick you up—was there a helper? Or the wife of the coach maybe? Anyone?"

Kylie shook her head.

"And you were totally fine? Like didn't cough, not even once?"

Again, she shook her head, her expression quickly transforming from mild annoyance to discomfort. "Dad, what's going on? You are being weird and it's making me nervous."

With every fiber of his being, he needed to shield his daughter from his panic. This was just some misunderstanding and she would be back any minute. Why worry her when he knew this would all work out soon? He forced a smile. "I think someone played a prank on mom. It was probably Tessa. I bet they are out to dinner now. She'll be home soon."

His daughter locked eyes with him for a moment. She muttered, "Okay," in that long drawn-out way that only teenagers and mildly irked people do and then turned back to her homework.

Shelley's phone rang several times as Lyle continued to call on repeat. No one picked up. After a few times, it started to go directly to voicemail. Lyle couldn't see where she was located using the app. Despite the fact that they had both shared their location with each other for years, hers was deactivated right now. It had never been deactivated. His anxiety skyrocketed at that point.

The clock said 9:04 PM. At 9:05 PM he would call. He watched as each second ticked by, hoping he'd hear the sound of the door open or her returning his phone call so he didn't have to reach out to the police. The clock clicked to 9:05 PM and he picked up the phone, dialing 9-1-1.

9-1-1: 9-1-1. What is your emergency?

Lyle: My wife is...she's missing. I think.

9-1-1: Okay, sir. Why do you think she's missing?

Lyle: Because she's not here! Sorry. Sorry. Um, she got a strange call.

9-1-1: Can you please elaborate? What was strange about the call?

Lyle: Someone called and said our daughter was sick and to pick her up—but she didn't pick up our daughter and she hasn't come back. She isn't picking up her phone and she turned off location sharing. Oh shit. Oh shit. I can't believe this is happening.

9-1-1: Sir, stay calm. How long has she been gone?

Lyle: At this point, over two hours. When I drove to get my daughter, I didn't see her car. It's pretty recognizable—a bright red convertible. I took a different way home and didn't see it then either. No one has heard from her. Her phone is going straight to voicemail now. Oh shit. Oh shit.

9-1-1: Okay, I need you to stay calm, Sir. I'll send an officer over now. Do you want me to stay on the phone with you until they get there?

Lyle: No, I think I'm okay.

9-1-1: Okay, I'm going to go. An officer is en route right now. They will be there in five to seven minutes.

Lyle: Thank you. Good night.

The phone slipped from Lyle's hands to the floor. His mind went blank as he looked straight ahead for several moments before snapping out of it. He knew he had to go talk to his daughter.

Chapter Five

LYLE WALKED BACK into Kylie's room. Her blonde hair was pulled up into a messy bun, little curls peeking out. She wore an oversized black sweatpants outfit. Her shoes looked like fuzzy slippers. When he was younger, this would have been considered a bedtime outfit but this is what kids called fashion these days. She had lined her green eyes with black eyeliner which she was definitely too young for, but he'd deal with that another time.

He had just told her that her mother would be fine, and now he was about to rip that false security away from her. How could she trust him anymore? That's what worried him most.

"Ky, we need to talk."

She turned around in the velvet pink chair. Tears were welling in her eyes and he wanted to say something to take away her pain. Though he knew that was impossible. The words he was about to speak were going to shred every bit of safety and security she felt. Neither of their lives would be the same after this moment. He picked up one of her figurines and started to fidget with it, not prepared to speak.

"I heard you," she wailed. "Why did you tell them before me?"

She got up and flung herself onto the bed, burying her head into the pink pillow.

He sat next to her on the bed rubbing her back in small and slow circles. Gus Gus must have sensed the distress because he pounced on the bed and nuzzled himself between the two of them. He could hear her muffled inhales and exhales as she cried softly. Her chest heaved in and out. He wanted to tell her it would all be okay, but was another lie worth the momentary comfort?

"An officer is coming to the house. They are going to help us find mom."

She flipped over in the bed and bolted upright. "I know you don't believe that. You think she's gone forever, don't you?"

"Kylie, I...to be honest, I don't know what is happening. All we know is mom got a strange call or at least said she did, and now she isn't here. But we are going to do everything we can to bring her home okay?"

"What does that mean—at least she said she did? Mom wouldn't just make something up...I mean, at least I don't think so." She turned her head away from him, as if looking away could change the landscape, change the situation.

Lyle was embarrassed that in this moment he had given a slight dig at his wife. He regretted it immediately. "I just meant, maybe she said that so she could get a second to herself. The police may want to talk to you. Okay? Whatever the police ask you, it's important that we try to remember everything we can so they have as much information as possible."

Kylie got out of bed and walked toward her desk. She picked up a fidget toy, spun it and watched it move around and around. "And we should be honest, right?"

"Of course."

Kylie lowered her head, still playing with the small toy, unable to meet her father's gaze. Her voice was just above a whisper. "Like, even about that guy she's been talking with?"

I was on Facebook last week and got a message from a high school acquaintance. I love how we are able to connect with people we haven't spoken to in forever. I feel like I talk to the same people all the time and it was nice to mix it up, talk about something other than PTA fundraisers or school drama.

Randy messaged me and was like, "Hey you were friends with my brother, right?". The high school version of myself would have been so excited- he was cute but he was a senior when I was a freshman. We chatted on messenger for hours.

I felt like I was back in high school, staying up way too late on the phone. He told me he was getting a divorce and hopefully I was a good 'shoulder' to lean on. And he listened to me talk about the baby in a way Lyle never has. He shared with me that he also lost a child and I felt bonded to him in that moment.

Even though it was just talking, I felt a little bit... I don't know- guilty? For talking to another man until 3am. There is no harm in just talking, right?

Lyle asked me why I slept so late this morning, asked if I was feeling sick. I told him I was up working on a project for the middle school social. I just couldn't admit why I was really tired...

Chapter Six

AT THAT MOMENT, the doorbell rang and with his anxiety sky high, the sound was like a stab to the heart. He had to put Kylie's revelation on the back burner, as much as it pained him to do so. He opened the door and the cold winter air poured in.

"Good evening. I'm from the Belmar Police," a man stated flatly. The officer, who introduced himself as Officer Clarkson, asked Lyle if they could talk inside.

"Can we talk out here?"

The officer eyes him suspiciously.

"I've got my twelve-year-old daughter in there and I'd rather not worry her."

The officer scanned Lyle's face for any signs of deception or nervousness. Then reluctantly agreed. He was much taller than Lyle's five-foot eleven frame and stood looming over him.

"So, tell me what's happening?"

Lyle frowned, appalled that this man was asking him so casually about this moment, the one that was tearing his daughter apart. The officer asked the question in the same tone a mechanic would if he brought his car into the shop for repairs. It disgusted him, but he pushed it down, needing to focus on Shelley.

Lyle recounted the story—carefully watching the officer's face to gauge his reaction. He knew he was suspect number one, regardless of the fact that he had been home the whole time. Each facial expression, each change in the tone of his voice, each body movement would be analyzed by the police. With that, they would pretty much decide what direction they wanted to take the case, and if they would focus their time on trying to find him guilty of her disappearance.

Lyle shoved his hands in the pockets of his jeans, trying to appear more laid-back. Then he thought better of it, thinking it made him look like he was trying to hide something. Shit, he thought, now it looks like I'm fidgeting. Being under a microscope only increased his anxiety and he felt awkward in his own skin.

"Any problems we should know about? Drug use?" Lyle must have looked shocked because Clarkson responded, "We just need to rule out any contributing factors, sir."

"Yeah, Okay. No, she definitely didn't use drugs. She was a PTA mom for God's sake."

"Drug addiction can happen to anyone," the officer replied as if doing a PSA commercial. "She have any affairs? Money trouble? Enemies?"

"There is nothing that would make Shelley leave," he lied.

"Any mental health issues?"

"She was seeing a therapist for a while but stopped not too long ago. The lady was off and then she just stopped responding. I think her name was Dr. Prince or Price."

"Was she depressed? Suicidal?"

It bothered Lyle that he asked these things so flippantly. Like he had become accustomed to doing, he pushed his anger aside.

"Look...she was overwhelmed. She was stressed," Lyle said purposely not answering the question, but also not lying.

The officer took notes on a small pad of paper. He looked up at Lyle when he was done writing and remarked, "Oh um...your eye." He pointed his pen towards Lyle.

His left eye began twitching rapidly, a nervous habit he always had. He covered it to shield the officer from the strange sight. "I must have gotten something in my eye, sorry."

The officer said, "You sure you're okay?"

Lyle nodded. He could tell the officer was trying not to stare at his eye. "I know this isn't easy right now but most missing people turn up in a few hours. The wait will feel like a long time but I'm sure she will be back soon. Maybe she just needed some fresh air. Give us a ring when you hear from her."

"Wait, but what about the phone call?" Lyle tried to protest. "It was strange. Doesn't that bother you? It was like someone was luring her out of the house."

"She could have made that up to give herself some time away. Like I said, give us a call when you hear from her."

"But what if I don't?"

"Forty-eight hours for a grown adult is the standard."

Lyle furrowed his brow in frustration. "Okay, thank you." He tried to hide the anger in his voice. They shook hands and Lyle walked into his too quiet house. He could feel her absence already.

I don't know how to help her. Yesterday she was beaming at Kylie's winter concert. Today I found her laying on the bathroom floor, crying, unable to catch her breath. I asked her what was wrong, and she said she didn't know. I asked again and she said, "That was the only time we will go to that 4th grade concert. It shouldn't have been..."

Some parts of me have sympathy for her, she's in anguish. And some parts of me are just so frustrated- how the hell can she go from happy to devastated without cause? I just want to yell at her to get her shit together. I laid with her for a while, on the bathroom floor. Didn't help. After a while I just said, "You need to talk to someone." She didn't respond...just kept crying on the floor. I had a house showing in 30 minutes, so I left her there. I have no idea how long she was on the floor.

When I got back home- it was like nothing had happened.

Chapter Seven

BY THE TIME the officer left, it was nearly 10pm. Lyle had recounted everything he knew but he was worried it wouldn't be enough. He plopped onto the couch, thankful for a moment of peace to try to process everything. Kylie must have heard him come in though, and his time to reflect was taken away from him.

"Dad, I don't think mom was happy."

He sat up, exhausted and overwhelmed. Somehow, he was able to muster the energy to engage with her now, because he knew she needed him in that moment. "Don't say that."

"I was mean to her. I hurt her feelings. Maybe she left because of me." She hung her head, both sad and embarrassed by her previous behavior.

"Look at me," he said lifting her chin. "Your mom loves you and she loves her life. She is happy. Like all of us, she has her moments. There are always a million things on her to-do list, there are always two places she needs to be at the same time. Life can be pretty demanding so she is often exhausted, but that doesn't make her unhappy." He kept eye contact with his daughter the whole time, so she could feel how sincerely he meant his words.

She got up from the couch, without a word, and returned with a book in her hand. He knew it well—it was the tan leather diary Shelley wrote in religiously. It was part of her nightly routine and helped sort out the ups and downs of everyday life. He might not have done everything perfectly as a husband, but he never broke her trust.

"We really can't be going through that. That's mom's personal thoughts. She didn't mean for anyone to see that."

Kylie tilted her head. "I already read it. While you were outside."

"Kylie," he said disapprovingly, but with the energy of someone who just completed a marathon. She flipped through the pages and Lyle sucked in a breath. *I guess we are doing this,* he thought, not a clue as to how much his wife exposed in those entries and if they were all appropriate for his pre-teen to see.

His daughter continued leafing through the pages, on a mission. She found the page she was looking for—written over and over in scarlet red ink Shelley had written: The pain of existence. That was it. Nothing more to clue them in on what exactly had been bothering her.

Lyle was unsure how to ask his next question and was afraid for the answer. "Kylie, you said mom was talking to someone. Do you know who?"

"Not really. They argued a bunch though. But I know it was some guy she knew from high school."

"And...he was her friend?"

Kylie drew back from him. "Dad! What are you asking me?"

"I'm just asking if he was just her friend." His voice feigned innocence.

"Ugh, I don't think she was doing anything wrong if that's what you are asking me. Gross! They just talked—but A LOT and like I said, it wasn't always nice. That's really all I know. I really don't want to talk to you about this right now!" Kylie got up abruptly and stormed off to her room, slamming the door behind her.

She left the diary open, the words searing into Lyle's mind. Had she been unhappy? Yes, there were times she was extremely unhappy but also times where she was brimming with life. In his mind, he always assumed it evened out.

The quiet and loneliness allowed him to absorb everything that had happened in the last few hours. As his mind wandered, he flipped through the pages skimming for anything else that jumped out. He closed the book, thinking how quickly their world had been turned upside down.

Lyle thought about how ridiculous it was, asking his daughter about her mother's relationship. It unsettled him how he had handled it and vowed to do better. How much could she really tell him? It's not as if Shelley was cheating, she would never have exposed her daughter to that. Lyle knew he'd have to learn more about this guy and how involved he was with his wife. At the thought, he could feel his stomach and fists clench in unison, as if partnered in a dance.

In the back of his mind, his thoughts started to morph. He wondered if maybe his wife hadn't been abducted. The mystery guy, the constant feeling of being overwhelmed...and these diary entries. Maybe she had left on her own free will. And if that was the case, he knew she'd just need a day or two to relax and then she'd come back home.

She loved him, and Kylie was her entire world. Lyle, who was used to de-compartmentalizing and blocking out negative emotions, locked into this theory. He subconsciously selected this less likely theory, because the pain of the alternative was unbearable.

He was confident he'd see his wife soon. With that delusion, he was able to close his eyes and drift off to sleep right there on the couch.

* * *

Excerpt from the personal diary of Shelley Lazrin, Dated March 2016

I can't even tell you what I'm doing right now—because I can't even explain it to myself. Lyle and I got into an argument. I started it. I can admit that. But sometimes I just feel like he doesn't see me. I am the wife, I am the mother. But I want to be Shelley too.

So, I just walked out, drove away and haven't stopped.

I've driven south for the last 4 hours. I think I'm in Virginia. I have no plan and only $45 in my wallet. My phone won't stop buzzing. I'm not sure what my next step is...and despite the fact that, I know it should be to call my husband back, I just can't.

* * *

Excerpt from the personal journal of Lyle Lazrin, Dated March 2016

That bitch.

Chapter Eight

"DAD! Wake up! It's 8:20! I'm late for school." And then her face lit up. "Or can I just stay home? Please!" she begged.

Lyle widened his eyes, still caught between sleep and being awake. "You gotta go to school, kiddo." He needed this time to try to figure out where Shelley was and convince her to come back home. Sure, they'd need a ton of therapy after this but nothing they couldn't handle.

Once the house was quiet, Lyle sat at the small kitchen table with his wife's diary. For the first time in years, he had to start the coffee machine. Shelley had a routine of waking up before him, starting the coffee and pouring him a cup when she heard the shower turn off. It was always waiting for him, piping hot, when he'd sleepily saunter into the kitchen. The simple act of love, a routine broken.

How many more simple moments would just break him? How many small acts did she do for him that intertwined into his daily life so much so that he took them for granted?

With slight hesitation, he opened the diary. Though he felt a little guilty, he rationalized that it was to help find her and bring her home. He read each page, a brief window into her thoughts for the day—the achievements, the boredom, the let downs.

Some of the days he remembered vividly—like when Kylie's team won the state championship last year and Shelley was so proud! She started to do a little dance as her daughter approached her and Kylie yelled at her to stop embarrassing her. She was so hurt by that. A moment she had hoped to celebrate with her daughter ended in rejection.

As his wife's thoughts came through with each page turn, it showed how she felt day by day. He saw it was an average life. Nothing stood out to him. Each page, he wondered when this guy that Kylie mentioned would come up, but there was none. Had Kylie been wrong? Or had Shelley decided that a journal without a lock on their bedroom nightstand wasn't the place to write about something so private.

After a few hours at the table, the coffee was long gone and he had read each word. He was no better off than a few hours ago. He looked at the time on the stove—he had another hour before Kylie would return from school.

Unable to sit still, he thought of what he could do next. It occurred to him to log onto their computer and look through her search history. If she went away for a few days, there would have to be some evidence here. Or maybe on her credit cards. Lyle had a lot more detective work to do and he was about to open her laptop when there was a pounding on his front door.

He scrambled to the front of the house. It was 2pm and he panicked. It could only be the police and they wouldn't have good news at this hour. Lyle slowly opened the door, not wanting to hear the news on the other side. Once the words were spoken that Shelley was hurt, or taken or worse...there would be no taking them back. They'd become reality—his reality, Kylie's reality.

"Let me into this goddamn house right now, Lyle!" Tessa.

A deep sigh escaped him. He didn't know whether or not he should be relieved that it wasn't the police or more stressed that it was her. He was running on fumes and couldn't handle the twister that Tessa brought with her everywhere she went; loud, impulsive, chaotic, destructive.

He'd never particularly liked her but he tolerated her for Shelley's sake. He was sure the feeling was mutual. "Hi Te—," he started but she cut him off.

"What the hell is going on? I haven't heard from Shelley in over twenty-four hours and she didn't show up for her appointment at the salon today."

"Jesus, Tessa. Calm yourself down. She can miss a hair appointment."

He noticed her dyed blonde hair still had the black roots showing so either she was so concerned about Shelley that she left the salon, or the stylist did a terrible job.

"Don't you tell me what to do! Do you know where she is? Do you!?" She was using her hands to emphasize her point, flailing them this way and that. Lyle stepped back to avoid an accidental collision.

"No, not at the moment." He dug his hands into the pocket of his jeans.

"Oh my God, Lyle," she said, rolling her eyes dramatically. "Then tell me why I should calm down?"

"Because she just needed some time to herself. She's fine and will be back soon."

"You don't seem to be too concerned that you have no fucking clue where your wife is. That's insane, Lyle." Then she cocked her head to the side and thought for a moment. "Oh shit. Is this about Randy?" Tessa started muttering expletives under her breath.

Lyle felt the embarrassment painting his cheeks red and anger bubbling up inside him. His mind fired off unconnected thoughts rapid and pounding like a summer fireworks display. It made him dizzy—did she leave on her own? Is she cheating? Or is she hurt? Is she leaving him? What about Kylie?

"Who the hell is this Randy?"

Tessa sighed. She asked to come in. Her demeanor changed, she was calmer, her tone softened. She looked at Lyle with a trace of pity. He wasn't sure if he hated that or was thankful she was talking to him normally.

Tessa sat on the recliner and Lyle sat on the couch opposite her. He gazed at her, waiting for the information that would probably tear down the one thing he thought was true about their marriage— they were committed to each other.

"Randy was…" she paused and shrugged. "Her new boyfriend? Maybe. I don't know. He went to our high school but graduated the year we got there. She never actually met up with him as far as I know. It was all online and on the phone."

He dropped his head into his palms, too mortified to look up. "How long has this been going on?" His muffled voice came through his hands.

"A little over a year. I'm sorry."

He looked up at her. "So, she's with him now?"

"Lyle, I have no idea. Like I said before, I haven't heard from her. I just think it's bad news if she's with him. From the stories she told me, he is unstable."

"Well then they sound perfect for each other!" Though he was just speaking from a place of anger, he knew he was out of line. He wished he could catch the words and reel them back in like a fish at sea.

"Asshole," she responded under her breath but intentionally loud enough so he could hear.

Lyle shook as he raged about his wife's infidelity, if you could even call it that. He hid his hands out of her view so she couldn't see them trembling. "So why was she talking to someone who was so unstable? That just doesn't seem like her."

Tessa bit her lip as she organized her thoughts. "Okay... so from what I know, it started off as harmless chat. The time spent talking got longer and more personal. They bonded, but he started to get forceful about meeting. I know it made her uncomfortable." Tessa sighed. "There was something else..."

Lyle raised his eyebrows, an invitation to continue.

"Shelley told me they bonded over the fact that they both lost a child. Except later, she found out he hadn't. All his kids are alive and well. Doesn't have custody of them though, no contact in fact. That's when she tried to cut it off, but he kept pursuing her."

"My god. That's awful," he said, completely stunned. "What else can you tell me?" Lyle begged.

"I would tell you more if I knew. All I know is his name is Randy, and emotionally they were close...until they weren't. But it was nothing physical. She does care about you, Lyle."

He looked at her with doubt and resentment. Tessa was treating him like a pathetic lost puppy. "Thanks so much Tessa. I'm glad to hear that my wife cared about me. Fuck! This is such a goddamn nightmare." He could feel his heart pounding rapidly. It sounded like a drum in his ears so he almost didn't hear her speak.

"Did you really not know about any of this?" And her face searched his for signs of guilt.

He stood up signaling their meeting was over. "I better get going."

"This is your house, Lyle. Just tell me to get out if you want me to go."

"I have a lot of work I need to do. My goal right now is to try to have her get in contact with us—even if it is just for Kylie's sake. If you hear from her..." and he almost couldn't get out the words, like his lips were holding them hostage. "Have her call her daughter." He walked out of the room without saying goodbye, leaving her there to escort herself out.

Lyle and I have been struggling to find our footing. We can have moments where we laugh and laugh, and others where we seem like strangers to each other, not being able to understand the other person's point of view. Sometimes I feel so disengaged from everything, including Lyle. And sometimes I feel so overwhelmed with love for him- but then I think maybe I'm forcing myself to feel this thing that isn't even there, simply because I want to be madly in love with him- even if I'm not.

I'm not sure if it is a blessing to bring us together, or another thing to cause cracks in our marriage but... I found out I'm pregnant and on Mother's Day too! We weren't even expecting it. I'm excited. Lyle's excited. Fingers crossed that we are bringing this baby into a happy and healthy home.

But excitement and fear are always intertwined. At least for me.

My greatest fear is I won't be a good mom and raise a good person.

Shelley's pregnant! I can't believe I'm going to be a dad. I was surprised at first- we hadn't even been trying.

We decided to start couple's therapy so hopefully the baby arrives in a better situation than we are in right now. We have to work past all our stuff- it's mostly her stuff to be honest. I feel great about the life we created but I worry she doesn't feel the same. I never know what I am going to get from her- sometimes hot, sometimes cold.

She just seems like she can't settle into anything, always looking for something beyond what we have here. She's trying to write a book but not sure if she will stick with it now. It's hard - I want her to be happy with all that we have, with all that we are.

But we both agreed to work on it for the baby. I've heard a baby makes marriages harder, not easier but I don't know- maybe we will be different.

Excerpt from the personal diary of Shelley Lazrin, Dated Jan 2013

I'm holding Kylie asleep in one arm and writing with the other so excuse the bad handwriting. Lyle and I are just so in love with this precious baby. We've gotten into a good rhythm and I'm finally feeling hopeful for the future. Maybe I need to see the future through someone else's eyes, someone else's potential to feel hope for my own.

I've seen us grow closer these past few months, working together as a team to take care of OUR baby. Watching him care for her has bonded me to him in a way that wasn't there before. I still can't believe I'm a mom! Arm's falling asleep...will write more later.

Chapter Nine

THE COMPUTER BUZZED as sunlight struggled to stream through the blue curtains. It didn't take long to hack into Shelley's computer. Her password was so predictable. He imagined himself scolding her about that and then wondered if he'd ever get the chance. The thought made pangs of pain pulse through his chest. Instinctively he began to ring his hands together in a fruitless effort to self-soothe.

He went to her messages on Facebook and there were several ones marked as unread- but no Randy. It was like he didn't even exist —or Shelley was really good at hiding her tracks.

Lyle began to open each message and read back as far as they would go—searching for any hint. He looked for signs that she was depressed, or planning to get away, or was in contact with someone sketchy.

He had no social media himself. He felt it was pretty phony and a huge time suck. His lack of experience made it hard to navigate at first but he got the hang of it. The search didn't yield anything helpful. Then he recalled an app or a website that had your messages disappear after being read. Maybe she had been using that to communicate with Randy.

Her messages showed she'd been chatting with a local woman. They were swapping local gossip, trading stories about their children. Shelley complained about how much driving she had to do for Kylie's basketball game. The woman responded that her child had early morning swim classes that were messing up her sleep schedule.

Looking through her search history, it showed she'd researched local painting classes and had booked one for a few weeks later. She bought a few new shirts from the Gap for both her and Kylie. She had done some searches for hikes in Hawaii. Shelley had posted a cute video of her and Kylie. It was a rare moment where their daughter was in good spirits and they attempted some TikTok trend, dancing in the living room while giggling. It was all evidence of a basic life.

The computer screen glowed and taunted him. *There is something here, you just have to find it*, it seemed to mock.

Lyle pounded his fist on the desk then regretted it, shaking out the pain.

A ding and a message in the corner popped up. It was from Shelley's mom.

Hi sweetie. Just checking in. Haven't heard from you in a while. He knew she had probably texted her first and then tried here. The last time he called his mother-in-law, he had just asked if she knew where she was, and then left it at that. He knew he needed to tell her, but he just couldn't bear to do it yet. Cowardly, he closed the website and left his mother-in-law in oblivion.

Excerpt from the personal diary of Shelley Lazrin, April 2020

Spring has sprung! It's like a light switch turned on and all the dead barren trees suddenly have these lush vibrant flowers. The temperature has warmed and the days are longer- and suddenly my mood lifted. I walked around reveling in it all and then a thought hit me- that all this would go as quickly as it came. The flowers will soon lose their petals and rot on the ground, revealing barren branches. A deep sadness overtook me and I crawled up under the shade of a tree and cried.

* * *

Excerpt from the personal journal of Lyle Lazrin, April 2020

Shelley told me about her walk today. Most wouldn't understand her reaction- but it was perfectly clear to me. Shelley is like the spring. Her vibrancy is always there, waiting for the long darkness to lift and for the beauty and life to emerge.

Chapter Ten

LYLE HAD CANCELED ALL his work obligations for today. He had a long to do list in his search to find Shelley. Despite the productive day, it hadn't yielded anything. He crossed off the last item with a forceful stroke of the pen. His journal was open, so he wrote:

Gone, day 3.

The frustration was screaming inside his body and he allowed to take over. He slammed the notebook shut and tossed the pen across the room.

His 3pm alarm went off.

With their recent arguments weighing on his mind, Lyle was eager for Kylie to come home. The stress of her mother's disappearance, vacation, whatever the hell was going on was causing them to take out their emotions on each other. They needed a reset and to find solace in each other.

He heard the motor of the school bus in the distance growing louder and closed his laptop, sprinting to meet her at the stop. A few kids got off and the doors began to shut. Lyle quickly advanced toward the bus and slammed on the door even as it had started to pull away.

The driver stopped and opened the door. "What are you doing?" he said angrily and then he saw the fear on Lyle's face. "What's wrong?" he asked in a nicer tone.

"My daughter, Kylie, she's supposed to be on the bus. Where is she?" he said breathlessly.

The driver's face started to mirror the alarm in Lyle's face. He called back to the remaining kids. "Anyone see Kylie?"

"She wasn't on the bus," a few kids hollered back.

After a beat the driver added, "Maybe after school activities?"

Without even responding Lyle turned around and raced toward his house, getting into his car. He sped away, ignoring the speed limit, making a beeline for the middle school. She never had basketball on Monday's so what other reason could she have for being at school still.

Lyle, on a mission, went straight to the main office. At the desk was the secretary. She sat with the phone to her ear. "Where is Kylie? Kylie Lazrin."

The secretary politely excused herself from the phone call. She stood, tugging down her green cardigan. The woman, seeing his panic, changed her voice from the phone call. It was now slow and calming, the way you'd talk to a baby before bedtime. "It's okay. What's going on, sir?"

"My daughter didn't get off the bus! She's gone." Lyle sank into the plastic chairs that were lined in front of her desk. This can't be happening, he thought to himself. The terror caused flashes of tension to pulsate through his body and his mind played tricks on him—going to the worst-case scenario and playing it over and over in his mind.

The secretary began typing on her computer. Her voice like a quiet summer night, "I'm sorry but she didn't come to school today. A message of her recorded absence was left on your phone."

He wanted to snap at this woman that he didn't get a call but then it occurred to him—it went to Shelley's phone.

He heard her call after him, "Do you want me to call the police?"

Once again, Lyle was on the move. Back in his car, he headed straight to the police station. The sun was starting to lower in the sky. As the light blue quickly morphed into a deep navy shade, his anxiety increased. Nothing good would come from Kylie being alone on a cold, dark night.

A young woman sat at the station counter. She opened her mouth but Lyle cut her off. "My daughter is missing. Her name is Kylie Lazrin. She's twelve, seventh grade. Curly blonde hair, green eyes. She didn't go to school today. I have no idea where she is. I need help finding her! Please!"

The chatter in the office was making his head buzz and it was hard to concentrate on what she was saying in response to his panicked plea.

Soon he was sitting at a table across from an officer who began to ask question after question. Lyle responded to the questions but was in another world. His leg shook so rapidly up and down that the officer couldn't keep eye contact with him.

"Has your daughter ever run away before?"

"What? No. Her mom is missing too and I'm terrified." Lyle felt his eye start to twitch. He lowered his head into his hands and took deep breaths until it settled enough to raise his head again.

The officer's entire body language transformed. His caring expression fell away and was now replaced with suspicion. "You have two people missing from your house...separately. And you haven't filed a missing person report on your wife?"

Lyle began to trip over his own words. "I—I had spoken to—I thought Tessa was going...she's not 'missing'. I think she ran off. There is a boyfriend." His words tumbled out disorganized like a child's overturned toy chest.

"Oh, good lord. Okay, I'm just here to take reports. I'm going to have to get you to sit down with the detectives. But we put out a BOLO for your daughter several minutes ago."

"A what—?"

"Be on the lookout—we sent her description to the local police departments."

The next fifteen minutes there stretched into an eternity as Lyle's mind cruelly projected unspeakable images. Suddenly he was snapped out of the nightmare. There was a buzz from the officer's walkie-talkie. Through the static he could make out what sounded like his daughter's name.

"Is she okay?" he shouted frantically to the officer's back. His heartbeat and breathing stopped momentarily, as if the whole world stopped and was waiting for the response.

The officer held up his hand in his direction signaling for quiet. He walked out the door and left Lyle with his thoughts, heavy and rapid like an avalanche.

The officer returned a few minutes later. "The good news is we found your daughter."

All the tension in his muscles released and he sighed deeply, feeling his heartbeat start to regulate.

The officer continued, "But we would like you to stay to discuss your wife. We don't have the grounds to keep you, but they'd really like to talk with you."

Lyle wanted to be reunited with Kylie first and promised to return early tomorrow morning.

His daughter was rebelling because she was in pain. He realized this, but she had scared the hell out of him and now the cops were up his ass. Lyle knew he needed to strike the right balance of being empathetic but stern.

When he saw his daughter's face turn the corner, all balance slipped away and he ran towards her. The relief he felt in that moment was like nothing he had ever felt before. He vowed to do everything he could to keep his daughter safe and try to bring her some semblance of peace during this chaotic time. Lyle rushed to her and wrapped his arms tightly around his daughter.

"She was walking along the beach. Found her all the way in Deal. She's pretty cold, wasn't wearing a jacket but other than that, fine." A voice in the distance said.

After a few moments, Kylie pulled away from her dad. "I'm sorry, Dad. I just..." tears were streaming down her face and he wiped one away with his thumb. "... I thought maybe I could find mom."

Lyle looked up to the ceiling to hold back the tears. He understood his daughter's need to do something, not just sit around and feel helpless. It's exactly how he had felt these past three days. He put his hand on her shoulder and gave it a little squeeze. "You walked over five miles from here? And without a coat? It's freezing out! I know you feel you need to help in some way but you should have told me. I was scared to death and it wasn't safe for you to go that far alone."

She hung her head. "I knew you wouldn't let me go."

"You're right, I wouldn't have. Don't do that again—it's incredibly dangerous. We have to let the police do their job and trust that they will find mom and she will come home. Okay?"

She nodded, a bit embarrassed and very shaken up.

"Let's figure out something we can do together. Put up flyers or something," Lyle said.

She agreed.

They turned to leave, his arm around his daughter as if he'd never let her go.

"Mr. Lazrin!"

Lyle turned.

"Tomorrow, 9am, here, okay?"

Lyle nodded his head. He had all night to practice his grieving husband performance for the cops. That should be just enough time.

Chapter Eleven

THE NEXT MORNING, Lyle sat across from the officers in a dimly lit room. The room was small and bare. The metal chair beneath him was cold and uncomfortable.

"I'm Detective Aaron Derzo," said the tall man, extending his hand to Lyle. Derzo's arms were as thick as basketballs and he shook Lyle's arm as if he were trying to pull it out of the socket.

Lyle worried he'd feel the sweat on his hands, so quickly wiped them on his pants before shaking the offered hand.

"And I'm Detective Trina Petrov. We will be working on your case," said the second officer. She had long red hair that was pulled back into a straight ponytail. Porcelain skin made her deep brown eyes pop, and they looked eagerly at Lyle.

Must be new on the job he thought.

Her petite frame almost looked comical compared to Derzo's tall, muscular build.

The two officers started by asking Lyle to recount the days leading up to his wife's disappearance. He spoke slowly and methodically. He had practiced what he'd say over and over last night.

"My wife is just—normal. I don't know how else to say it. She loves her daughter and is involved in all her activities. We love each other. But there were stressors—the ones we all have—too busy, not enough money. Normal stuff."

"What isn't normal is that a man's wife goes missing and he doesn't bother to file a missing person report. He doesn't ask friends and family to look for her. That's not normal, right, Lyle?" Derzo asked self-assuredly.

"How would I know what's normal? I've never had a missing wife before," he lied. He thought back to the body language research he had done last night and ran through the list of signs a person is lying. He played them in the back of his mind, making sure he wasn't exhibiting the tell-tale markers of a liar.

"Check your records. I did call the night she went missing. The officer blew it off and said she would come back on her own. Said just call back when you find her. She didn't come back but as you can imagine, I didn't feel like I'd be taken seriously after that." *Make eye contact, don't touch my mouth, stay calm and still in my seat,* he reminded himself.

"But she's been gone four days now," Petrov said meekly.

"That's a long time to not call," added Derzo.

He wondered if they too had practiced what they would say, as if they were all in a play, each person making up their own lines as they went along.

Lyle didn't respond.

"What do you think happened to Shelley?" asked Detective Petrov softly.

He had the sense that they were playing the classic good cop, bad cop routine and he shouldn't trust either of them. Lyle rubbed his eyebrows and then quickly lowered his hands back into his lap. "I think she needs a few minutes to cool off."

Petrov piped up, "Cool off from what? What was going on between the two of you?"

Lyle thought for a moment, trying to organize his thoughts. "She just felt stressed. That's all I know. She will be back soon."

Petrov let a small, "Mmm hmmm," slip from her lips.

Detective Derzo raised his eyebrows. "She's been gone four days. How long before you were going to be concerned for your wife?"

"I am concerned. Very." Lyle felt himself losing control of the conversation and he went into fight or flight mode. He had to grip the chair to stop himself from getting up and running from the room. *Stay calm*, he repeated to himself.

"Doesn't seem like it. You didn't make any effort to find your wife!"

"Yes, I did," Lyle snapped.

Lyle realized that he shook his head from side to side as he said this, and quickly glanced at the officers who were looking at each other. He imagined them silently saying, *"We got him."*

"She could be dead by now," Derzo pressed, intentionally trying to rattle him.

Lyle's eyes widened in shock. "You know what? Fuck you! That's it. I'm done. I'm done! If you aren't holding me here, I'm going home."

"At this point, you are free to go. But we will be looking for your wife. And we will find out who took her and we will see that they are punished to the fullest extent of the law," Derzo said.

"Listen—I just found out my wife has been talking to some guy. And apparently, he's bad news. Maybe look into that."

Lyle stood up. He swore he saw Derzo mouth, "Motive," to Petrov and she gave a little shrug.

The police didn't have anything on him and he was free to go. There was no point in trying to talk with these two if they already assumed he had something to do with it. Angrily, he pushed his chair back under the table, but he pushed too hard, rocking the table. The two officers glared at each other, more convinced than before that they were on the right track.

There was no putting it off any longer. While sitting in his car, he dialed his in-laws.

"Hello?" came his father-in-law's voice, deep and raspy.

"It's Lyle. Is Linda with you? I need to talk to you both."

He could hear his father-in-law yell for Linda.

"Oh Lyle, what's going on? I haven't heard from Shelley in days."

"Linda, I'm so sorry. I just hoped this would have worked out and didn't want to worry you..."

"Say what you need to say!" his father-in-law interrupted, his interjection like a clap of thunder.

"Shelley's missing," he said delicately.

He heard Linda gasp and the increasingly distant. "No...no...no."

He was now only speaking to Tom, Linda's wails heard in the background.

"What do you mean missing? For how long?"

"She's been gone four days. I'm so sorry. I was trying to say earlier why I waited."

"My god." The line went quiet for a few minutes. "Okay, we are going to come up this weekend—we need to take care of a few things first."

"Like what," he asked, trying to keep the curiosity out of his voice.

"Well, first we need to tell Joshua. Oh god, how do we tell him his sister is missing?" Linda's wails became louder. There was a pause and a long exhale. "We might fly out to Chicago to tell him in person. I'm not sure. I need to talk to Linda and as you can hear she isn't in a state to discuss that right now."

"Right," Lyle said.

"And we need to meet with the police. Contact the media."

Lyle didn't know what to make of that comment.

"We need to do everything to find her," Tom stated.

"Yes, I agree. But get here as soon as you can—I think Kylie could use your support right now. She—we—miss Shelley and it's been difficult to say the least."

He could hear Linda's anguished crying in the distance as they said goodbye and hung up.

. . .

Tessa sat across from the two detectives. Her frame took up most of the seat and she could feel the metal handles pressing into her. "How inclusive," she grumbled to herself. Petrov's bright red hair was the only source of color in the depressing room. Tessa held back from commenting that they could spruce the place up a little bit, add some color. But as usual, she couldn't hold back everything. "You could get chairs that weren't just for women that are a size two," she complained as she tried to get comfortable in the seat.

The detectives just nodded and apologized.

There was one goal with today's visit; let the police know her insights into the situation. There were things that Lyle just wouldn't bring up. Without that information, they may never find Shelley—or whatever happened to her.

Detective Petrov placed a bottle of water in front of her and took out a notebook. Her demeanor was warm and Tessa started to feel her muscles relax a bit more.

"Thank you for coming down to talk with us today. Why don't you start wherever you'd like and we will interject if we have any questions. Sound good?"

"I never liked Lyle," Tessa said matter of factly, looking straight at the detectives.

Petrov looked up from her notebook, taken aback by her frankness. "Really? Seems like a likable guy."

"Yeah, he's fine I suppose. They just weren't a good fit. Shelley probably never should have married, never should have had kids. It's not that she was a bad mom or wife, but she just never should have tied herself down to one house, one job, one life path set in stone. It just wasn't her. And over time I think Lyle pressed her to be what he needed or what the world expected of a wife, and it only felt like a heavier weight on her. She was a butterfly with clipped wings."

"What was her job?"

"A bunch of broken dreams. She dabbled in many things but

nothing panned out. I guess you'd say she was a housewife but she'd never call herself that. More like an 'aspiring...insert current goal'. Shelley probably had six different jobs on and off since we graduated. I think she felt a little resentful that none of those goals or jobs panned out."

Detective Derzo glanced over at his partner and they silently spoke to each other in a language Tessa couldn't speak. Did she drop a bombshell? Or did they not believe her?

Derzo asked, "So, was the marriage rocky because of this? Was she resentful toward Lyle or Kylie...or both?"

"Somewhat. But at the same time, she knew she chose this. And she loved them both, don't get me wrong. But she always felt like she was slowly drowning, slowly suffocating to death."

"How was your relationship with her?" asked Petrov.

For some reason, Tessa wasn't expecting that question and her surprise showed on her face. "It was great. We were close friends," she said defensively.

"How about her other friendships?"

"As far as I know, everyone liked her. She was nice as can be. Always the first to help with anything needed at the school. People appreciated her."

Derzo wrote in his small notebook: "Used past tense." It was flat on the table so Tessa could clearly see it. A surge of panic rushed through her.

Derzo asked if Tessa felt her friend was at risk for taking her own life.

Tessa didn't miss a beat. "Not a chance. Listen, this may not make sense to you, but it did to her. She both loved her family and was struggling. Both things can be true. A person can be two things at once."

"What about running away? Lyle mentioned there was another guy."

She shook her head. "I thought maybe it was possible at first. But the more I think about it, I just don't see it. I think the last thing she would try to do was jump into another marital strangulation."

Derzo pulled back, shocked by her dramatic words.

Petrov stopped writing for a moment and locked eyes with Tessa. "So, what's your gut telling you happened to your best friend, Tessa?"

"The husband did it. Always."

Chapter Twelve

WHEN KYLIE GOT HOME, she yelled for her dad as she slammed the front door. He was supposed to pick her up from basketball practice later today so he was surprised to hear her voice. She tossed her backpack onto the floor with a thud.

"Kylie, why aren't you still at school?"

"I don't give a shit about basketball," she barked.

"Watch your language, please."

"No!" she shouted. "I don't give a shit about any of those kids or the coach. The whole team is a bunch of morons."

Lyle reached out to hug his daughter, knowing whatever this outburst was, came from a place of hurting. She quickly pulled away. For now, he needed to help her ride the wave of this negative emotion. He'd deal with the inappropriate language later.

"Sit down and let's talk about it." He patted the couch and she sat close to him.

Before he could even ask again what happened, she was sniffling into his shirt.

"Tessa's daughter told the team Mom was gone and to be nice to me because I wasn't in a good place, or something like that. But do you think they did that? No! Lilly walked right up to me with her stupid smug face and said mom was probably off screwing someone. And then Piper said you probably killed her!!! That bitch!"

Lyle knew he should reprimand his daughter for using that language, but Piper was kind of a bitch, even though she was only twelve. He'd let this one slide. He made a mental note to add *"Thinking a middle schooler is the B word"* to his next confessional, though he had no clue when he'd find time for that.

Kylie was wailing uncontrollably now. The weight of everything was too much to bear and she crumbled to pieces. She dug her head into his shoulder and he wrapped his arm around her. Her small frame heaved from the overwhelming emotion and he could feel her tears wetting his shirt.

"I don't want to go back there. I don't want to be anywhere."

That was a stab to the heart. "Please don't talk like that," he said, feeling his throat constrict.

Lyle thought about how he would need to reach out to the guidance counselor. He'd give his daughter all the support he could, but she needed far more than he was capable of.

He wanted to tell her everything was going to be okay because as a parent that's what you do; make everything okay. But was it?

Chapter Thirteen

LYLE THOUGHT BEING proactive would help him and his daughter to process their emotions, or at least give the constant buzz of anxiety an outlet. He arranged for several close friends and family to arrive at his house. Standing on his front lawn, he held a large stack of missing flyers waiting for people to arrive.

His in-laws stood by his side. His father-in-law stood tall and firm, supporting his wife who looked like her spark had been fully extinguished. She looked a decade older than the last time they saw each other. Her hair, which had been salt and pepper, was now fully white. As always, it was nicely styled.

Once the crowd had fully assembled, Lyle cleared his throat. "I want to thank everyone for coming out this morning. Shelley has been missing for over a week now and we need to get the word out so that we can bring her home. We all miss her and just need her back now." A rock formed in his throat. His father-in-law nodded in approval as his mother-in-law continued to look out into the distance.

Kylie stood next to him and reached for his hand. He gave hers a small squeeze as tears streamed down her face. He could feel her trembling and he wasn't sure if it was from being in front of a large crowd, the cold ocean breeze, or from the pain of her mother's absence.

Lyle began to dole out directions—where each person would go, how to hang the flyers properly, and to talk to people along the way to bring attention to the situation. He added that if anyone had any information, to use the contact information at the bottom.

His in-laws took their flyers and left him to continue to manage the crowd.

Tessa pushed through the mass of people and approached him for her stack. She examined them with a strange look on her face.

"What?" he asked turning to give another stack to the person beside her.

She shook her head and continued to look at the photos.

"What?!" he repeated.

"God damn Lyle. Why did you pick the worst pictures of her?" The next person in line gave her a quizzical look before heading off with their papers.

Lyle drew back, shocked at her words. He looked at the poster, the first picture of her on Christmas morning at Lyle's family get together, tired but happy with Kylie. The middle photo was her driver's license picture, Lyle assumed using an official government photo was a good idea. The final image was the last one he took of her. She was having her morning coffee on the couch. Sure, she wasn't made up, but he loved how the light danced on her face that morning. She was so lovely that he couldn't help but snap a picture with his phone. He recalled her being happy that day, happy that she had the morning free to drink her coffee and read. She was beautiful in all of them, he thought.

Lyle let the spew of hatred he wanted to say run through his mind. Once he ran through it all and felt satisfied, he took a small breath before saying, "As always, thanks for your help, Tessa. I'm sure Shelley would have appreciated you being here."

Tessa rolled her eyes and stalked off with her doormat of a husband following behind her while she still grumbled about the photos. Lyle could overhear him say, "She looks fine. Leave him alone."

Each person got a stack of fifty flyers and was sent on their way. Lyle and Kylie stuck together and walked along the boardwalk.

An officer approached them after they had hung several flyers. "You can't post these here."

Lyle furrowed his brow. "I'm sorry officer, another one of your colleagues told us we could."

"They gave you the wrong info. Not on the boardwalk. Take them down please. You can post them on the side streets."

Deflated, they went back, tore down each poster and moved to another location. It was odd that he had been told that he couldn't hang them here he thought. He was positive that the detective had said he could when he discussed the plan. He wondered if that officer didn't want people knowing about the case or maybe it went higher up—like the posters of a missing mother might negatively reflect on the peaceful image of the town.

They turned off Ocean Avenue and walked along 10th street in silence. Kylie held the poster in place on the telephone poles while Lyle stapled them in and then on to the next, creating their own little assembly line. He wanted to say something to her, but didn't know what would help in that moment. She was his baby, his one and only child. How could he help take away her pain?

As they pinned up the last poster, he was still trying to find the perfect words.

"Can we go home now?" she asked solemnly.

He felt like a failure of a parent. In forty minutes of walking around together, he couldn't think of a single thing to say to soothe the wounds.

"Sure, kiddo. Hey, do you want to grab something from the Windmill? Fries? Hot dog?"

She shook her head. "I couldn't possibly eat right now."

"Right, yeah, sorry. That was a dumb thing to ask."

And they continued on in silence, Lyle cursing his stupidity in his head the whole way back.

Chapter Fourteen

SHELLEY'S PARENTS drove up again from Cherry Hill for the day. From all their conversations so far, they seemed to support him. For the first time, he was actually looking forward to seeing his in-laws. He had few people on his side at this point and it would be nice to be around someone who didn't side eye him suspiciously.

Linda, his mother-in-law, got out of the car and looked better than she had yesterday.

"Hi, Bubbe!" Kylie said, hugging her grandmother.

Lyle noticed Linda holding the hug a little longer than usual, knowing that Kylie was the best link to her missing daughter.

Lyle embraced his mother-in-law, and she immediately began to cry.

"I can't go on without knowing where my Shelley is."

"I know. We are going to find her." He pulled away from the embrace so they could be eye to eye. He placed one arm on each of her shoulders. "We will find her, okay?"

She continued to cry but she nodded in agreement.

Tom, Shelley's father, stood back, taking it all in. He was still as stoic as he had always been. Not everything was the same though.

He watched his wife more carefully now, as if she was a delicate object that could shatter at any moment.

"Hey, Tom," Lyle said to his father-in-law.

Tom just nodded.

They all sat in the living room, not knowing what to say in this unfamiliar territory. Normally Shelley guided the conversation and without her there to start things off, a silence overtook the room. Everyone felt too awkward to pierce the quiet. Linda began to tear up again and pulled a Kleenex from her bag, soaking up the tears.

"You told Joshua?"

Linda closed her eyes and tears flowed like little streams down her face. She spoke so softly that Lyle had to lean in to hear her. "Yes, he's absolutely heartbroken he couldn't help with the flyers but he can't get away from work right now."

"I understand. This is a busy time of year for him." Lyle tried to find something else to say. "Kylie, why don't you tell your grandparents about basketball?"

She just shook her head. The awkwardness was almost unbearable and Lyle shifted in his seat. Linda continued to cry while Kylie looked on the verge of tears. Lyle looked at his watch. "Well, I better get going. Thanks for watching Kylie," he said.

Lyle got a call to come down to the station early that morning. Linda and Tom offered to stay with Kylie while he was there. The short drive over, took an eternity. There could be news at that station that could make his world crumble. He had convinced himself that Shelley was alive and working through something. Each hour that went by, though, started to chip away at that conviction.

Every second he put off going to meet with the officers, could delay hearing a truth he couldn't handle. For a split second, he thought about stopping by Driftwood Coffee for a caffeine boost, or maybe it was just to have a few extra moments in this existence—the one where Shelley needed a break. But then he realized that he'd look pretty guilty if he showed up late with a latte so he continued on. Being under a microscope made him doubt everything he did and it was mentally exhausting.

At the station, he was escorted back to a small and barren room. He held his breath, hoping this would pause time. Lyle let out a sigh and then asked, "Did the flyers lead to any tips?"

Derzo shook his head. "Lyle, we brought you down here today because we have an update. We found your wife's car at the Newark airport."

His whole body morphed. A long slow exhale escaped him and his muscles relaxed. "Thank God. So, do you know where she went? She really wanted to visit Hawaii."

Detective Petrov sucked in her lower lip. "I'm sorry to tell you this, but she didn't go away. We checked the flight records and there were no passengers with her name flying anytime since she disappeared. And there was blood in the car," Petrov said calmly.

"Wait…what are you telling me?" he said, his voice full of confusion.

This time Derzo spoke. "Unfortunately, we think it is likely that your wife met with foul play."

Lyle began to frantically shake his head back and forth, as if he was a magic 8 ball trying to get a new response. "No, no, no. Check the other local airports. Maybe she went to Philly or JFK. She likes to travel." He was speaking quickly, at the same rate as his rapid heartbeat.

"We already did. Your wife didn't fly from any local airports. Listen, we are going to need you to stay here for questioning. Take a second to arrange care for your daughter, you'll be here awhile."

"She's with my in-laws."

Their life together, with its ups and downs, flashed before his eyes. The proposal at Grounds for Sculpture at sunset. Trying to slide the wedding ring on her finger but being so nervous he dropped it into the grass. Awkwardly trying to figure out the car seat for the first time as she stood behind him in the parking lot, holding their wailing daughter. Sitting hand in hand at their daughter's first dance recital, beaming at her. Parent teacher conferences, listening to teachers year after year saying Kylie was bright but a bit too talkative.

The second child that never was.

Her heartbreak.

And her heartbreak.

And her heartbreak.

Excerpt from the personal diary of Shelley Lazrin, April 2023

The pen is heavy in my hand. How can I even write this?

I lost the baby last night. I was 7 weeks along. I hadn't even gotten a chance to tell Lyle. I took the test and then I started bleeding hours later while he was at work- I was a mom of two for a few hours. There was a baby inside of me, a hope for a future. An extra hand to hold. Now there is nothing but emptiness and unfulfilled potential. Will every moment going forward be filled with the world going on around me, while I'm stuck imagining a child that never was, never will be...

* * *

Excerpt from the personal journal of Lyle Lazrin, April 2023

How the hell am I supposed to handle this news? Shelley told me in the same breath that she was pregnant and that she lost the baby. I just don't even know how to process it.

She was looking at me like I should be feeling more, but I didn't. She became angry and I just flipped. Like, who is she to yell at me about how I am supposed to feel?

I never yell or get angry at her for all her god damn ups and downs but she flips on me if I don't react the way she wants me to. Lord knows, I could for all the drama she's brought into this house.

"Lyle?" Petrov asked.

"Yeah, sorry," he said, trying to clear his head and focus on the moment.

Answering their questions was like stepping around landmines. They had their problems, like most couples. He couldn't decide if it was better to lie and make their marriage look perfect. If they found out later, which they almost surely would, he could never regain their trust. Any slight variation from the truth could make them laser focused on him. Or should he tell the truth and have them think he had a motive?

"How did you feel about your wife? And your relationship?"

Lyle rubbed his forehead so forcefully it was like he was trying scrape it away and then he shrugged. "I loved her...and I hated her."

Petrov looked up sharply at that. She tried to force down a smile.

Lyle immediately regretted going with the honesty route. Clearly Petrov was giddy, thinking she had caught him in this moment. But what could he do? They were going to go through his text messages; his browser history; talk to his friends and family. It would all come out eventually.

Detective Derzo tried to catch Petrov's eye but she had locked her gaze on Lyle and wouldn't let go so he looked back to Lyle. "So, tell us about the good days."

"You don't want to hear about that. You want to know why I hated her so let's just skip to that." Working in Real Estate, Lyle made enough BS conversations trying to land a sale and just wanted to get to what they wanted to hear so he could go back home to Kylie.

Derzo shrugged, so he took this as permission to do as he wished. "Shelley was always caught between two places—wanting to be what the world expected of her as a mother, a wife, and a woman, and wanting to be what she saw in herself.

"And she could never get those two things to co-exist. I loved her for all that she had in her, her passions, her quirks...but that wasn't enough for her. And she struggled with feeling like we weighed her down, held her back...and I hated her for that. For always wanting and expecting something that just wasn't there. That our life together was never enough for her."

Spent from the entire exchange, Lyle turned his head to the side, no longer able to meet their gaze. He knew they must be judging him —what kind of asshole said things like this about his wife? His *missing* wife? Sure, he joked with friends about what a pain Shelley could be, sure his daughter had heard him raise his voice in frustration with her, begging her to just be happy with the life they had. People could see the small cracks but they thought it mirrored their own issues. Lyle had never fully articulated aloud the complexity of their existence. Now it was just hanging in the air, growing stale.

"Listen, I understand why you think I had something to do with this...but I don't know what happened or where Shelley is." Their suspicious glares were irking the hell out of Lyle but he knew he needed to keep calm and focused. "But you know what I do know? That I have a twelve-year-old daughter at home who is absolutely destroyed by the fact that she doesn't have her mother there to ask her how her school day was, or to braid her hair in the morning."

The two officers sat across from him, unmoved by his plea. He continued anyway, "I need you to help me, to help us, find my wife. We need her home." His voice cracked at the end as a single tear escaped and he quickly wiped it away.

Petrov looked away, visibly uncomfortable with his emotions.

Lyle didn't know what else to say, what else to do. All he could do was beg for their help, and after that he was at their mercy.

Detective Derzo stared at Lyle with cold blank eyes. "You were the last person to see your wife alive. The truth is—we know you did it. You were the only person with means, motive, and opportunity."

Time slowed as he tried to process those words. "I—," Lyle started to respond but Derzo raised his hand, silently signaling for Lyle to shut up, which he did.

Detective Petrov pushed her long red hair behind her ears. She locked her brown eyes on him. Her voice was soft like a summer breeze rustling tree leaves. "You killed your wife. You know it, we know it, everyone in your life is going to know it soon too. Now we just have to prove it."

Chapter Fifteen

IT HAD BEEN hours of grueling interrogation and he was starting to feel delirious. Lyle begged to be able to go home and see his daughter before she had to go to bed. To his surprise, they agreed and Lyle walked out into the cool night. He drove with the windows down, letting the fresh air revive him.

Lyle gripped the doorknob and turned it without resistance. When he walked in the door, Kylie was on the couch, fully asleep still in her clothes. He placed a kiss on her head and she stirred. Despite this loving exchange, he couldn't help but be annoyed at her carelessness. "Kylie! I told you to always lock the door, but especially when I am not home."

Kylie gave him that familiar look, the one where she looked at him like he had two heads.

"I'm serious! It's not safe to keep it unlocked at night, even with your grandparents here."

"Dad, I locked the door! I always do. I do listen when you tell me to do something, ya know."

"Well, I was just able to walk in here and if I can, so can anyone else. Please, please double check it next time."

Lyle made a mental note to check later if the lock was broken or loose. Then he thought he'd better add some additional security around the house. One could never be too cautious. Completely exhausted, he quickly thanked his in-laws and asked if they could speak outside for a moment before heading home.

"What is it?" Linda asked. He told them what the police had found and Linda crumbled like a house of cards in the wind. Tom escorted his wife to the car, practically having to carry her.

"Are you sure you don't want to stay?"

Tom just shook his head as he continued to the car, Linda's arm draped around him for support.

When he reentered the home, his daughter adjusted herself, standing a bit taller, so she was looking directly at him. "You can tell me. I think I'm ready to hear the truth."

"Ky…I don't know what you m—" he started to say.

"If she's not coming home, tell me."

"The truth is, they don't know." He began to wring his hands nervously. The anxiety was causing him to collect nervous tics as if they were trading cards. He was terrified to tell her the rest of what he knew. "They found her car at the airport. The police, well I don't think, that they think, she's coming home. But what do they know? No one really knows, we just have to keep the faith and pray for a good outcome."

"Maybe she went on a trip." Her eyes were begging him to tell her that everything would be okay.

"Anything is possible."

He could see in her expression that she wanted to say something but was holding back. Lyle gave her a small smile to encourage her to speak her mind.

"She loved me, right?" Her voice, normally so full of confidence, was weak and pleading.

Lyle pulled his daughter into him. "She loved you so, so much. She'd always say you were just the most perfect thing ever created. And I like to think she felt the same about me," he said, forcing a smile with no emotion behind it at his sweet, heartbroken daughter.

"If that's true, then she didn't leave. She's gone, Dad." Her lips pulled into a straight line, barely visible.

Lyle closed his eyes and let a small breath slip out. Though all the signs had been there, these words from his daughter tore down his delusional facade. For the first time, he saw a life with just the two of them, and he cried with his daughter for the wife he likely wouldn't see again, for the life that no longer existed, and could no longer be repaired.

* * *

Though he hadn't been much of a runner, Lyle felt the overwhelming urge to go out and run like hell. After Kylie had been dropped off at school, he threw on some gym clothes and laced up his old sneakers. He double...and then triple checked that he locked the door behind himself.

He blasted loud music into his ears and as soon as his feet hit the pavement, he ran faster than he ever had before. The sensation made him feel like he was flying and he could briefly imagine he was floating away from the absurdity of his current situation. The blood pumping through his veins and the music in his ears, made him be able to feel more strongly all the things he had pushed down.

Not used to exerting himself this much though, he quickly became out of breath. His chest heaved and his lungs stung from the cold air. The muscles in his leg began to tense. Everything hurt.

As his pace slowed, he was able to take in his surroundings more. He began to walk and with each telephone pole that he passed, he became unsettled but unsure why at first. And then it hit him...the posters that they had just hung up. Where were they? He hadn't passed a single one.

Lyle sat down on the curb, exhausted both physically and emotionally. He couldn't figure out why anyone would want to take down the posters of a missing local mother. The idea disgusted and angered him. Some people were just so vile, he thought.

A man walking a large dog approached and the dog pulled him toward Lyle. Normally a dog lover, he couldn't handle any extra stimulation right now. As the dog lunged and growled in his direction, Lyle barked at the man, "Keep your damn dog away from me."

The man looked shocked. "Jesus, chill out...hey wait, aren't you that guy who..."

Lyle stood up, ignoring the pain as adrenaline pumped through his veins. "Who what, asshole?" He puffed out his chest.

The man tossed his hands up to indicate he hadn't meant anything by it, clearly not ready for a brawl on his morning walk with the dog.

"That's what I thought!" Lyle yelled after him.

The man picked up his pace, trying to get away as quickly as possible.

After a minute, Lyle calmed down and realized that in fact, *he* had been the asshole. He was having a hard time recognizing himself. The stress was invading every part of his body and was making him someone he didn't like.

Lyle pulled out his cell phone and dialed the police station. He left a message with Derzo. "It's Lyle...all the flyers have been taken down. Can you look into who might be taking them down...please?" Maybe this was a blessing in disguise. Maybe whoever was taking them down knew more about Shelley's disappearance.

Chapter Sixteen

April 2025

JUST BEHIND HIM, the waves rolled in fiercely. Lyle stood on the boardwalk with a novice reporter in front of him. She had her hair slung back in a low ponytail and wore a thick pink cardigan. The microphone she held looked ridiculously large on her small frame.

There was so much riding on this interview and he knew the public would pick it apart. The public would decide if Shelley was worth looking for like they do for all victims. So, in addition to trying to get the word out, you have to convince the public that your loved one's backstory is compelling. Because if not, screw them, they can stay missing.

This was just a part of the disgusting reality. Lyle knew Shelley was beautiful but she had to be the right type of beautiful. It was the young girl next door look they wanted. Everyone had to see Shelley as their own mother, sister, best friend. The whole thing made him sick and he started to feel liquid rise up in his throat, acidic and hot.

Instinctively his cheeks puffed out and he hunched his shoulders, trying to push the sensation back down.

It wasn't just Shelley that needed to catch their attention. Lyle needed to be the perfect balance too. Likable, but not too outgoing. Concerned and upset, but at just the exact measurement—except the measurement wasn't known; it was just felt later. There had to be sadness and a touch of anger but also a good dose of hope.

All this caused an avalanche of anxiety when the reporter said, "Ready?" And she began to address the camera man before he could even reply that he needed a minute.

"Good morning! I am Rebecca Avos with KTT news. We are in Belmar, New Jersey reporting on the case of the missing mother and wife, Shelley Lazrin. Sadly, Shelley went missing in March and has yet to be located. I have her husband, Lyle, here with me today. Lyle, can you tell me a little about Shelley." She spoke in that self-assured intonation that all reporters used.

Lyle's stomach lurched, and he could barely think. "Shelley is…" oh God, he felt so sick. "A great mother and wife. She has many…" He paused, not because he was at a loss for words, but he feared what was about to come out of his mouth.

A breeze blew and it carried the smell of the pizza parlor down the street. It made his stomach flip flop.

Too many beats went by so the reporter, what was her name again? encouraged him to continue. The sound of the waves felt like his stomach, going up and down, in and out. Lyle placed one hand over his stomach. The reporter narrowed her brow, trying to figure out what was happening with him.

Get yourself together, he thought. "She has many great passions. Like painting. And…." He couldn't keep it down any longer, on live television, he leaned over the boardwalk railing and threw up onto the sand below. It seemed like several minutes, in which they must have been recording his backside, convulsing.

When he turned around, he wiped his mouth with his hand.

There would be nothing more satisfying than running away right now.

"You um, have something right there," said the reporter, pointing to his chin.

They were still recording as Lyle, on live television, wiped yellow vomit from his face. Though the reporter looked embarrassed for him, there was no stopping live TV so she cleared her throat and pulled herself together. She went on as if nothing had happened.

"Can you please tell us what you think happened to your wife?"

Lyle's eyes widened, shocked that she thought the interview would continue.

"I think I better go," he said and he began to walk away, toward his home. Each step quicker than the last.

He could hear her shout, "Lyle! Lyle! Do you have a message for your wife?"

He desperately wanted to shout back, 'Fuck you!' As a message to the reporter, but then that would be twisted to be interpreted as his message for Shelley, shown many times over as a sound bite. Lyle speed walked back to his house, hoping they weren't following behind him.

Chapter Seventeen

IT ONLY TOOK ABOUT thirty minutes for his phone to blow up with text messages from his friends.

Xavier: You okay man?

Mason: You looked real smooth on TV today.

I didn't know about Shelley. I'm sorry. Came a message from a friend he hadn't spoken to in years.

Let me know if we can help in any way.

That was a train wreck, man. You better stay in hiding for a while.

Maybe don't do live interviews again.

He wanted to crawl under a rock and hide forever, or at least until some other guy made a bigger fool of himself. People's attention span was short and they would move on, he just had to ride out the next few days under the radar.

The stress was zapping all energy from him and he laid down on the couch to close his eyes for just a moment.

He was awoken by Kylie flinging the door open and screaming. Lyle jolted up from the couch. He knew this sound well, not the scream of someone in danger or scared, but a pre-teen pissed off. He tried to greet her but he couldn't even get the words out.

She tossed her backpack on the floor and screamed, "I hate you!" as she ran towards her bedroom, slamming the door. Her cries could be heard through the house.

He wasn't sure what exactly had set her off but he gave her a few minutes to cool down. When enough time had passed, he knocked softly on the door. No answer. He knocked again. No answer. "Kylie, can you please let me in."

She didn't respond but he heard a click on the other side unlocking the door.

As her father, he had watched her struggle through some of the difficulties that this age brought. Some he could relate to, some not so much. There had been ups and downs with friends, the crush of not making the softball team when every single one of her other friends did, the high of later making the basketball team, hating boys, liking boys. Her life was constantly cycling between two worlds —childhood and adulthood. He knew it was difficult as it was, and now she'd have to navigate some of these important moments without her mother. It was a lot for one child and he wished he could make it better for her.

"I'm sorry you are upset. What's going on?"

"You! You ruined my life. Your interview today went viral and—"

"Viral? Come on, it's just a local news station. Just a few people probably saw it."

"A few? Try 10,000 views on this short."

"What? How is that possible?"

"Dad, this isn't the Stone Age. Kids have phones, they are usually on them during most of the day."

"But they are supposed to be in class."

Kylie just rolled her eyes, thinking his reaction was too naïve to even bother responding. She pulled out her phone, tapped a few times and then turned the phone to him.

Lyle's mouth hung open as he watched the short clip play over and over. Someone had taken the video of him vomiting and overlaid the words 'Think he did it?' And after he wipes away the vomit, it switches to a meme of a child laughing maniacally.

"Oh, my…God." He ran his hand down his face.

"Yeah," she said sarcastically.

The video had creeped to over 15,000 views after being posted only two hours ago. He watched as the view count ticked up a few more each second, his eyes widening in horror. It felt like every part of him was rattling, like a leaky pipe about to burst.

"You know I am never going to school again, right? Like I can't, Dad. I just can't."

He reached to put his arm around his daughter but she pulled away.

"Tell me I don't have to go to school again, Please." Her eyes were pleading with him.

Lyle bit on his lower lip for a second and then ran his hands through his black hair. "Let's just take this one day at a time. You can stay home tomorrow. I'll email your teachers."

"I'm absolutely beat. I'm going to go to bed." She pulled back the covers on her bed and crawled under them.

"Kylie, it's only half past three."

"I just need to escape. I just want to sleep." Kylie reached for a stuffed rabbit, that she pulled into her chest.

He leaned in to kiss her forehead and she didn't move away. "Good night. Love you."

She just muttered something and then turned to her other side, tossing the blanket over her head to block out the afternoon light. She created a cocoon of both warmth and darkness. For now, he would let her shut out everything. Eventually they would have to face what lay ahead of them and learn to cope but today wasn't that day.

Chapter Eighteen

WHEN HIS PHONE had buzzed in Lyle's pocket, he had been surprised to see it was the local police. They had called to tell him that they wanted him to come down to review some doorbell camera footage. For the first time, since she disappeared three weeks ago, he felt a tiny spark of hope. Whoever they saw on the recording could have answers as to what happened to his wife. In the back of his mind, he was convinced he'd see this Randy character.

"Sit down," Derzo said to him.

Lyle pulled out the chair and leaned forward, eager to see what they had.

Derzo flipped the laptop toward Lyle and pressed play.

Lyle grabbed the laptop and pulled it closer. He squinted as he tried to make out the grainy footage. The first few clips were too hard to make out. "Looks like a woman," he observed. "That's really all I can make out."

Derzo nodded.

They flipped to the next clip. "Oh, my god!" Lyle exclaimed as it switched to another camera which had a much better angle. "That's..." and he couldn't even form the words. There on the screen was Tessa, angrily tearing down a poster, crumbling it into a ball and shoving it into the large tote bag she carried.

When the footage stopped rolling, he looked up at Derzo. "I don't understand."

"Can you tell us who you think that is?"

"It's clearly Tessa. But why? She's her best friend."

Derzo shrugged his shoulders. "We just received this footage from a few people on 11th Ave and wanted to have you review it too. Get your feedback. Any reason why she'd be taking down the posters?"

Lyle tried to think of a reason but nothing came to mind. He knew she had been a pain in the ass at the event but Tessa was always that way. "No," he said shaking his head. "Absolutely nothing that I can think of. Like I said, they were best friends."

Nothing made sense to Lyle anymore. Nothing he thought to be true was true. It was disorienting. His wife wasn't the faithful partner he thought her to be. Her best friend clearly wasn't the fearless advocate for Shelley that she had presented herself as. Lyle felt like he was moments away from losing all grip on reality. How can he keep his sanity if everything made him feel like he was going insane?

"So, what now?" he asked.

"We will bring her in and get her side of the story," Petrov replied. "But for now, why don't you tell us a little about their relationship?"

"They've been friends since before we even met. I think, sometime in elementary school. I'm not the biggest fan of her—she's too loud for me, but I've never heard a complaint from Shelley about her. She found her antics amusing. They were good friends and spent a lot of time together." Lyle shrugged his shoulders unsure of what else to say.

"Do you think she could have hurt your wife?" Derzo asked.

Lyle thought for a moment. "No, I don't. But lately I feel like I don't know a damn thing about anyone and it's driving me crazy."

Chapter Nineteen

LYLE constantly worried if he was doing the right thing for Kylie. She barely left her room and he was going to give her space. But maybe he should go and talk to her? When she would emerge, she moved slowly, like a deflating balloon. Maybe he should do something to cheer her up? Or was that insensitive given the circumstances?

While he was lost in thought, she walked up to him at his desk. "Did you take my photo album? The one mom made me for Hanukkah last year?"

Lyle shook his head. "I wouldn't take anything from you without asking."

Kylie's face looked alarmed. "It was on my desk last night. I was looking at pictures of me and mom. It's not there anymore."

"Maybe the cat knocked it over?"

"Seriously? I checked the floor too, Dad. Last I checked, Gus Gus doesn't have opposable thumbs and the desire to reminisce about the good times."

He knew sometimes his daughter could miss things right in front of her face so he looked around but didn't see it either. Lyle racked his brain for a logical explanation but he couldn't arrive at one. He wanted to call the cops—maybe someone had broken in. But how would it look that he called sooner about a missing photo album than about his own missing wife?

"It will show up, sometimes things just get misplaced. Our minds are all over the place right now. Remember that time mom lost her keys for three days, and she found them in the freezer? You probably put it somewhere silly without even thinking about it."

She nodded slowly. "Yeah, maybe you're right."

* * *

Tessa had been called down to the police station and she immediately noticed the officers' demeanor had changed from the last time she was here. She kept scanning their faces for any hint of what was to come. She was worried that they knew what she had done but maybe they just needed to ask her more questions. Tessa stifled her nerves and played it cool. She smiled at them, trying to be charming but couldn't help but shift a little in her seat. Portray confidence she thought to herself.

"So did you get any evidence on Lyle?" she asked self-assuredly.

"Ms. Guillino, we wanted you to look at some footage," Derzo said as he started typing into his laptop.

Tessa froze momentarily.

Petrov's eyes were locked on Tessa, assessing her every move.

Shit, shit, shit, thought Tessa. It was nearly impossible to keep her wits about her when she knew what they were about to show her. *Why did everyone need a goddamn camera attached to their house?* she fumed to herself.

Derzo turned the laptop around and pressed play. There she was, shot after shot, tearing down the missing person flyers. Her unmistakable bright blonde hair with its black roots was one give away. She realized she was wearing the same Eagles hoodie now that was in the recordings. *How could she be so stupid?* she lamented to herself.

"It's not a crime to tear down paper," she said trying to sound confident but it just came across as shifty.

"Yes, we understand that," said Petrov, who then leaned back in her chair.

Derzo, in turn, leaned into Tessa. "But why would a person who is grieving, take DOWN the posters of her missing friend? Do you not want her to be found?"

Tessa thought for a moment, if she should ask for a lawyer. *No,* she thought, *they are just asking me about some papers. It would make me look worse if I lawyered up over something so stupid.* Tessa decided to take back control of the situation, so instead of cowering to Derzo, she leaned right back into him. It was like they were dancing, and in her mind, Tessa was always the leader. "Did you see the photos he picked?"

The two officers nodded, unsure of what she was going to say.

She stared them down. "And don't you find anything funny about them?"

Derzo raised his eyebrows. When she didn't continue, he said, "No."

"Well, I did." Tessa felt the confidence coming back and she was definitely in control again. "He literally picked the worst photos of her...he did it on purpose. You both know that image is so important to getting anyone to care about your case. So why would he pick these shitty pictures? Because he didn't want anyone to care! And then they won't look for her. So that's why I took them down." And Tessa smiled at them cockily.

She noticed that both officers ever so slightly shook their heads, like they couldn't believe her explanation. Undeterred, she continued, "What cases can anyone unfamiliar with true crime rattle off? Most of them are young and blonde and they are always pretty."

"Are you a big fan of true crime?"

"Jesus, Mary, and Joseph! Is that a real question? Like every woman I know is obsessed with true crime. It's like a suburban woman starter kit—red wine, sweatpants, book clubs, a to-do list that never ends and true crime podcasts. Listen, I don't care what you think, I know he did this." She then leaned back into her chair, exasperated that her speech hadn't swayed them.

Derzo seemed unimpressed with her reasoning. "Well Ms. Guillino, maybe you should care what we think. Because it makes you look like someone who could have been involved in the disappearance of her, supposed, best friend."

Tessa scrunched her face as if to say, 'Oh come on!' She leaned in further to the officers. "Whatever you are insinuating; I didn't kill my best friend." And as she made this proclamation, she pulled the dark green strings of her hoodie, trying to hide the scratch marks on her neck.

Chapter Twenty

IT HAD BEEN a month since Shelley had left the house and not returned. Though it was difficult, Lyle was trying to give Kylie some semblance of normalcy. She had a basketball game this evening and he was happy to go support her. Kylie reluctantly stayed on the team after her coach spoke with her. In the end, it was proving to be a good distraction for her. Lyle could see a bit more fire in her moves lately and he wondered if it was like a therapy session for her, channeling her anger into dodging other players, pounding the ball into the wooden floor.

The game started and Kylie was on the bench. He watched the game but if she wasn't out there, he'd pull out his phone from time to time.

There was a text from an unknown number: **It's all going to be okay, Love.**

What the hell, thought Lyle. And then his muscles froze. He thought of how badly this would make him look and hoped no one nearby saw his screen. This looked exactly like what the cops would want to find on his phone, like he was having some sort of an affair.

Quickly he typed back: **Sorry, wrong number.**

Kylie was just bouncing on to the court. Normally he wouldn't take out his phone while she was playing but just to be sure, he flipped on the phone so he could block the number. As he was doing that, another message appeared at the top:

It's not the wrong number, Lyle.

The cheers and jumping fans around him went into slow motion. His eyes darted around the room as he could feel the blood pumping through his veins.

Had anyone seen what was written?

As he scanned the room, Lyle's eyes met the gaze of another father. The man, who he didn't know and was wearing the opposing team's gold and green logo on his shirt, started to mimic Lyle's interview debacle. He was holding his stomach and pretending to retch. The men around him laughed, like the high school bullies they must have been. Someone else saw this and did the same, causing more laughter. He felt like the entire room was looking and laughing at him.

His body froze except for his eyes which continued to dart around the room.

He took a deep breath and paused, knowing his immediate reaction to yell, 'Fuck all of you!' would just lead to another viral moment. So, Lyle sat there, stewing in his own anger and embarrassment. He rapidly tapped his fingers on his thigh, another nervous tick added to his collection. Without the satisfaction of a reaction, the taunts died down but his anger remained like an ominous cloud. Now he just prayed that Kylie was focused on the game and didn't notice.

With the sound of the buzzer, Kylie's team won, and though it was immature, Lyle took that as a defeat over the parents on the other team. He climbed down the bleachers, several eyes on him as he passed families. Ignoring them, he went to congratulate his daughter.

"We won!" she shouted.

He was relieved to see that she seemed like herself and was in good spirits. *Thank God,* he thought, assuming she didn't notice.

On the drive back home, she sat beside him, her phone lighting up the whole car with a soft glow. "I'm going to quit basketball."

Lyle was surprised to hear this after their big win. However, he had too much going on to have this battle with her right now. "I thought things were getting better. Take a day to think about it before you tell the coach. At the end of the day, it's your choice and you should really only do the things you enjoy."

"Piper told me it was distracting having someone like me on the team." She said it nonchalantly but he knew those words must have stung immensely.

"Yeah, well you can tell Piper to—" and he caught himself. "You can tell Piper that if she doesn't have anything nice to say, she shouldn't say anything at all."

She agreed to talk it over with her coach before making a final decision and went back to scrolling endlessly on the phone, nothing holding her attention.

The next morning, Kylie implored her dad to keep her home. She drew out the word 'please' like it had five syllables.

"Ky, if I keep you home too many days, I think they can make you repeat the grade."

She went through a litany of reasons, and it became background noise as he kept thinking back to that text from the game. Who the hell had sent that text?

"So, can I?"

"Yeah, yeah sure," he said before realizing he agreed to let her stay home again.

"Thanks, Dad!"

With his mind back on the conversation he added, "But if you do stay home, no cell phone time. You can read and rest. Catch up on any missed work if you need to." He worried that she was using the phone more and more to escape into a digital world so she could leave behind this one of pain and uncertainty. It wasn't healthy.

As predicted, she moaned and groaned, hoping if she made a big enough scene he would relent.

"That's the rules. You make your choice. I'll say nothing more about it."

Lyle had always been the more firm parent, so she quickly realized her complaints were being unheard. So, Kylie went off to school, grumbling to herself the whole way there.

Lyle sat in the Wawa parking lot. Fear kept him in the car. He just didn't know who he would run into there. But he also desperately wanted a strong coffee. Unfortunately, he could no longer go to his favorite spot where they knew his name and order. He tossed on a hoodie and pulled the strings tight, covering a good bit of his face. The thought occurred to him to add sunglasses but thought better of it—he didn't need to look like he was robbing the place.

Incognito, he walked in cautiously, scanning the store to see if he knew anyone. He quickly filled up the 24oz cup with piping hot coffee, grabbed some sugar and creamers and did the automatic check out. The less interaction the better.

Once he got to his car, he just sat there, hoodie still covering his face while he slowly sipped his coffee. He was alone with his thoughts. All the things he could have done, should have done, pounded away at him. It was like a tsunami and he found himself gasping for air.

There was so much that he wished he did differently. He should have been more empathetic. He should have let his wife know that he was there for her, no matter what mood she was in, regardless if it was convenient for him at the time or not. He let her emotions moor her out to sea without a lifeline.

He went into what he could only consider a trance at that thought. Lyle was completely still, as cars came in and out of the parking lot. The world going about its day while he was frozen in time and place.

Regardless of what happened to his wife, he would always feel responsible for the fact that she never felt the love she deserved in their time together. He thought back to their last really good moment on the beach, watching the sun transform the sky briefly into a pastel masterpiece and then how quickly it had been taken away by a cloud.

Lyle just sat there, coffee growing cold, for an hour with his wishes and wants for a second chance.

Finally, he gathered himself together and went home. The now freezing coffee got tossed into the garbage. He went to his bedroom, hoping to nap the day away but was immediately taken back...his room was different.

Lyle stood there, processing everything. The photo frames on the nightstand were empty. There had been two frames—one of their wedding day and one of Kylie's latest school photo. Gone.

Frantically, he continued to move around the room. The things of value, like the TV, were still there. Shelley's diamond earrings, a tenth anniversary gift, were still in the box on the nightstand. He pulled open the drawer of the nightstand, the box that held her wedding ring was missing.

He walked into the closet, the right side filled partially with his clothes and shoes. The left side, however, was completely bare, leaving a huge void that had been filled with all of Shelley's belongings. His first reaction was that he was going crazy, imagining the impossible. He went to her section and waved his hands around frantically, hoping he'd feel them there. But of course, nothing.

He moved quickly around the house to see what else was missing. Nothing but the photos, the ring, and clothes. Lyle briefly thought that this was a sign she had come back. That theory didn't last long though, she would have left a note—a reason for her absence, a message for her daughter reassuring her that none of this was her fault and that she was still deeply loved. He was sure of that.

But if she didn't take out her belongings—who did? And why?

And then fear struck Lyle like a lightning bolt. When the cops came to look around the house, they would think Lyle had gotten rid of every trace of Shelley. And it would be just another tally mark in their book that he had caused her to go missing.

Lyle was so angry that he started punching the door as he screamed a string of expletives. When his anger subsided, a large punch mark through their bedroom door still remained.

He was now a man with a missing wife, all her belongings discarded and the remnants of a violent outburst.

* * *

Excerpt from the personal diary of Shelley Lazrin, November 2024

We were all home today, with not much going on. But with a full house, I still felt incredibly alone. Kylie's in her room, not wanting to interact with either of us. Lyle's been in the office for hours working on God knows what. How do you tell your spouse that even when you are together, you feel so incredibly lonely at times? And that the loneliness physically hurts?

Chapter Twenty-One

KYLIE SAT in her last period class, tapping her pencil on the desk staring into space. She twirled her hair around her finger so tightly that the tip turned white.

Her teacher approached her. "Kylie?"

Kylie shook her head, snapping out of her thoughts, that were miles away from this, and bringing her back into the classroom.

"Kylie," the teacher, Ms. Santoro, repeated softly. "Class ended a few minutes ago. Are you..." the teacher paused, knowing that asking her if she was okay was a ridiculous question. "Do you need to talk?"

Her first reaction was to push the idea away, rejecting help as people often automatically do even when they desperately need it. She allowed herself to be vulnerable. "Yeah, I think I do," she said quietly.

The teacher sat down at the desk next to her, her adult frame filling up most of the space. "You seemed like you were somewhere else. Do you want to tell me what you were thinking about?" the teacher asked gently, allowing her to guide the conversation.

She wasn't sure how much to share with her teacher but once she started speaking, the words and emotions flowed from her uncontrollably like a babbling stream. Kylie averted her eyes from her teacher's caring glare, afraid of any reaction—sympathy, surprise, anger. No matter what it was, she just couldn't handle it right now.

It ached to be in her own skin and she pulled on her sleeves creating a cocoon around herself. "I don't know how to navigate this situation. I feel a hole in my life from the absence of my mother, but when I try to imagine how things could play out…you know what most people think happened…I can't go there. The pain of never seeing her again is too vast, too great for me to even be able to wrap my head around. How can I go the rest of my life without my mother? How can I go another day without her putting her arms around me and telling me that she is proud of me. I miss things I never noticed—the smell of her vanilla perfume, the way she left out snacks on the table ready for me when I got home from school. You never think about how many simple acts are proclamations of love."

Her teacher was taken aback by the beauty of her words. She thought of the small things she did for her students every day and how yes, they were little acts of love. She wanted to reach for the girl to show her how much she cared but hesitated.

Kylie lowered her head onto the desk and began to sob. "I want my mom," she said over and over through tears.

Her teacher moved the desk closer and, now too moved to hold back, placed her hand on her back and rubbed gently.

As a teacher she had dealt with students in a variety of difficult situations, but never anything like this. She knew nothing would take away her pain, that she just needed to let time very, very, slowly chip away at the grief until it wasn't a boundless ocean but more like a large, tumultuous, lake.

When Kylie lifted her head, Ms. Santoro got up to hand her a tissue, to wipe away the mascara that was dripping like little black rivers down her cheeks. "I'm here for you anytime you need to talk," was all she could finally offer. At least that was true she thought to herself. She was opposed to the nonsense most people fling at people wading through grief.

"Do you know what they are saying about me?"

Her teacher shook her head uncomfortably, though she had some idea because her students were loud and had no filter. However, she definitely didn't want to say it out loud.

Kylie blotted her eyes again with the tissue. "They say my dad did it. That I'm living with a murderer."

Her teacher, like most of the town, also assumed this was the case, or at least the most likely scenario. "I think the police are working really hard to find your mom, Kylie. No one knows what happened, not even the police at this point."

Kylie nodded.

"No matter what happens, we want to find your mom, so let's focus on that for now. We can only work with the information we have—and all we know is she needs to be found."

"Yeah. I guess that's true. Thanks for talking with me, Ms. Santoro."

She placed her hand on top of Kylie's. "Anytime. Seriously, anytime." Ms. Santoro put on a facade of strength, knowing as soon as her student left, she'd break down for the sweet girl who laid her pain before her so expressively. Teaching had always come easy to her, but navigating students' trauma was always a challenge.

Kylie stood and slung her backpack over her shoulder. She forced a smile at her teacher, thankful for her kindness and attention. She walked out of the door to her classroom, closing it gently behind her. As she turned toward the main entrance of the school, she noticed something shiny. Laying there on the ground was something that caught her eye.

*That couldn't be...*she thought. She picked it up and flipped the locket over. Engraved into the back was her name and birthdate, a gift her dad had given her mom shortly after she was born. Goose-bumps ran down her arms and her whole body shivered.

She looked side to side down each wing of the hallway, scanning to see who was there. Given that class had let out thirty minutes ago and there were no clubs today, the hallway was silent and empty. Kylie shoved the necklace into her pocket with a deeply unsettling feeling.

She ran into the bathroom, shut the stall and sunk onto the ground. Kylie examined the necklace. It was definitely her mom's. She held it, squeezing tightly to the small object as if it was her mother, because right now it was her only connection to her. "Mom, why is this here?" she whispered. She waited desperately for a sign, any signal from her mother. When none came, she got off the dirty tile floor and put the locket back in her pocket.

The walk home would take twenty minutes and she was fearful of being alone. She thought about calling her dad to pick her up but thought she was over-reacting. Kylie knew she couldn't act like there was a monster lurking around every corner for the rest of her life. She still had to live.

As she walked into the cold air, she bundled up her black jacket and trudged down the steps. A gust of wind made her shiver and she started to reconsider calling her dad.

A police officer was sitting in the car at the base of the steps. When Kylie got near it, the window rolled down.

"Kylie?" asked the officer.

Panic struck her and the world froze. "Yes…" she said slowly.

"Hi, I'm Detective Petrov. I'm working on your mom's case."

"Just tell me," she blurted out.

A moment of confusion flashed over Petrov's face and then she realized what the young girl must be thinking. "No, no… sweetheart, it's not like that. I was just here interviewing staff. I know your mom was very involved in the PTA and had interactions with many of the teachers here. I was just trying to gain some extra information. It's late to be getting out of school, is everything okay?"

Kylie nodded and explained why she was still at school.

"Would you like a ride? It's really nasty out today."

Kylie paused for a moment, not eager to get in the car with a stranger but it was a police officer. As a strong burst of wind whipped her face, causing her hair to fly in all directions, she decided to hop in. They drove along, the hum of a local radio station playing pop music.

"Did you find anything?"

"What do you mean?" Petrov asked.

"Did you find any information about my mom...at the school?"

"Oh, sorry. No. No new leads there, unfortunately. But we will keep looking, sweetheart. You must be very proud of your mother. She really does a lot at the school. All the teachers had really great things to say about her. I even got to see a photo of the amazing spread she set up for teacher appreciation week. The social studies teacher said they ate like royalty." Petrov looked at her and gave a smile.

Kylie realized she was probably waiting for a response but all she could feel was this guilt pushing down on her. The overwhelming regret. "She is pretty amazing." And she forced a smile back, despite not having anything to smile about right now.

In between the two seats, Kylie noticed an old flip phone. "That looks like it belongs in the antique store," she quipped.

Petrov laughed a little too loudly.

"Can I see it? Does it play that game snake my dad always tells me about?"

Petrov reached for the phone and put it in her shirt pocket. "Sorry, that's my work phone. They don't give us phones that are mini computers like you have there." She looked over at Kylie and smiled.

When they pulled up to the house, Petrov said to Kylie, "If there is anything you need to tell us, we are available to talk to you at any time. If there is anything that could help us find your mom, please let us know as soon as possible. We want her home as much as you do."

The detective put her hand on Kylie's shoulder and smiled at her.

She thanked her for the ride and then dashed into her house, ready to ball up in her room and have a good cry.

When Kylie woke, she realized she had fallen asleep in her clothes. The necklace was still in her pocket. She held it out, examining it again with intense curiosity. Finding the necklace brought her warmth—it was an unexpected connection to her mother. It also brought intense fear—like someone was trying to send her an ominous message that they were watching her.

She opened the locket and gasped. Instead of being the small photo of mother and daughter, there was a white paper with handwriting. It said, "Love, Mama." Kylie had never called her mother that—and this wasn't her handwriting.

A soft knock on her door jolted her out of her thoughts. "Yeah!?" she called shakily while shoving the necklace into her pocket again.

"Can I come in, kiddo?"

"Uh...sure."

Lyle entered the room and looked at her quizzically. "What's the matter? Looks like you saw a ghost." As soon as the words floated through the air, he knew he had said something incredibly stupid and insensitive. He sat on the bed. "Shit, I'm sorry. That was such a moronic thing to say."

"Dad, it's okay...I know you didn't mean anything by it."

He reached his hand out and she took it.

Kylie felt the necklace in her pocket more intensely now that her father was next to her, like a burning secret pressed to her body. She sat up in bed. "I have to tell you something but don't freak out."

"Never a good way to start a conversation with your parent, but go on..."

"Seriously, if you want me to tell you, you have to promise to stay calm." And she held out her pinky.

He looped his pinky around hers and they shook.

"Okay, so yesterday I stayed after school for a bit...and when I left my class, mom's necklace was on the ground, right by the room I was in. The photo is gone and someone wrote Love, Mama inside. I think it's trying to send me a message and I'm scared. Like what if I'm next?" She was filled with grief, anxiety, and loneliness. "Who would do something so sick?" she asked her father. "And how did they get the necklace? How did they know where to find me? What if they are still watching me now?"

After Kylie went to bed, Lyle thought about the necklace. There was only one explanation—whoever took Shelley had to have had access to the school too. And the only person Shelley knew who had access to the school were her friends on the PTA...

Chapter Twenty-Two

THERE WAS a knock on the door and Lyle felt a sudden pang of discomfort as his stomach clenched. There was no chance someone at his door could be good news—police, reporters, those damn soulless true crime podcasters. Who knew? but it wouldn't be anyone he wanted to see. He prayed, if it was the police, that they didn't have a warrant to enter the home.

To his surprise, it was the postal worker. He felt a moment of relief until he noticed her expression. She looked displeased. How he had managed to piss off the mail carrier too was beyond him.

She stood with a large, disorganized stack of mail in her arms and a grimace on her face. "You haven't been taking your mail out of your box and now I can't even fit in the items still coming in." She pushed the large stack of envelopes into his arms.

"Sorry, lot going on right now," he tried to explain to the unfriendly woman.

"Yeah, don't we all got a lot going on." She shook her head and rolled her eyes.

"Won't happen again." He flashed a large sparkling smile as a peace offering.

She turned without another word.

Lyle dumped the massive pile onto the small kitchen table. Gus Gus began rubbing against his leg as he flipped through, sorting junk mail from bills. "Not now!" he bellowed but the cat didn't seem to heed his request. There was a red card, with no return address. He inspected it—suspicious since none of them had a birthday coming up. The postmark was from Belmar, so it had been sent locally.

He turned the card over and the front cover was a cat laying in a hammock. Quirky for sure. He melted a bit, thinking this might be a sign from Shelley. They had this inside joke of giving each other greeting cards for the wrong holidays and then writing a silly message inside. A quick memory popped into his mind—the time this tradition started.

Shelley had nearly forgotten their eighth anniversary and ran to the dollar store to get a card. They were all out of anniversary cards so she grabbed a happy eighth birthday princess card. Inside she wrote: 'Can you tell I waited until the last minute?' After that, they tried to one up each other with more ridiculous cards every year.

He could feel the blood pulsing through his veins from the excitement of having something tangible from his wife, a sign that she might be okay.

Inside the card had pre-printed, 'You're purrrfect.' His name was printed on the top. The bottom just said, Love. He dropped the card on the table like it was a hot coal. What the hell was happening? "God damn it!" he shouted into the room. This wasn't Shelley's handwriting.

The missing album, the text, the missing clothing and now this card. It was like someone was watching him and following him. He knew he needed to talk to the police but was apprehensive about how they would react.

Chapter Twenty-Three

AT THE KITCHEN TABLE, Lyle had his phone, laptop, and a notepad. While the office would be more comfortable, he just couldn't bring himself to work in that space. It made him think of all the time his wife had spent working in there and he wanted to imagine that she was still there, typing away.

Sometimes, he imagined himself asking, "Hey, whatcha working on?" Such a simple question to show he wanted to know more about the things that were important to her, but he was too focused on himself.

Sitting at the kitchen table, Lyle found the first contact he wanted to reach out to. He had shown an out of town couple a little run-down house that they had hoped to fix up and use as a rental. The rentals during the short yet busy summer were enough to pay the house expenses for the entire year. Couples looking to add to their wealth found these a promising investment.

The wife picked up after two rings. "Hello?"

"Hi! Erica! This is Lyle from Beach—"

"Hold on a second," she interrupted.

Soon a much deeper voice responded. "Yeah, hi, we've um

decided to go with another realtor. We are signing on another property tomorrow, actually."

Lyle's face went red. "Sure," he said curtly and hung up the phone without a goodbye.

He spent the next two hours trying to make calls—and they all went the same way. When he got to the bottom of his list, a young man picked up.

"Hello?"

"Yes, is Anya available?"

"Who is calling?"

"This is Lyle Lazrin from Beach Front Properties."

"Sorry if I am off base here but aren't you that guy whose wife is missing?"

Lyle was already boiling as he went down the list of names unsuccessfully and this was his tipping point. He slammed the phone on to the table.

"FUCCCCCCK," he roared. He could hear the muffled, "Hello? Hello?" coming from the phone. He had forgotten to hang up.

He tossed the phone across the room and, as it landed with a thud, he prayed he hadn't cracked the screen. There was no money for a new one. It was like his body was being overtaken by rage and he just yelled until every ounce of energy had left him.

In just a short time, he had to process the disappearance of his wife, supporting his daughter through her grief and now the complete lack of income. He just couldn't see what he even had left to live for at this point, other than his daughter.

His smart watch dinged and he saw a notification that the TV bill was past due. Earlier he'd gotten an email that the electric bill was due tomorrow. They had enough money for now but how much longer could they get by without income? Three...four months tops. He had never felt so hopeless.

Lyle thought about canceling their trip to Hawaii, getting back some of the funds. Shelley had worked hours and hours planning it.

Though the money was needed, he just couldn't bring himself to do it—not yet.

Gus Gus approached him and he picked up the ginger cat. He transported the cat to the bedroom and, petting his soft fur, gave him a much-needed moment of calm. There, they slept the day away. While he knew it didn't solve anything, he didn't care. Sleeping was an escape from all the problems and the mounting bills.

Chapter Twenty-Four

THE NEXT WEEKEND, Lyle's in-laws came for a visit. With his new role as a single parent, he was thankful to have other adults around, even if it was just for the day. Linda got right into asking about the investigation and Lyle noticed his father-in-law shift in his seat.

"Do we have to do this now, Linda? We just got here."

"It's been over a month! When else would be a good time to talk about this, Tom?"

His father-in-law stood up. "Kylie, care to walk the boardwalk with me? I'll get you a smoothie if you'd like," her grandfather asked. He had never seemed comfortable with big displays of emotion and Linda was always on the verge of tears talking about Shelley. Kylie got up also eager to leave the situation.

Alone, Lyle offered to make his mother-in-law some coffee and they moved to the kitchen. They spoke of the investigation for several minutes but there wasn't much new to discuss.

"How is Kylie holding up?" she asked.

"All things considered, she's managing. I think part of us is in denial about what is happening. At some point we will slam into the reality of this situation like a brick wall, and just shatter."

Linda lowered her head and sucked in a breath. She slowly released it. "I'm terrified for that moment too. You know we support you, Lyle."

"Tom doesn't seem to. He hasn't even said a word to me today."

"No, no, it's not like that. The more time that passes, the more he fades away. He's only half here right now. The other half is in his head, trying to understand what happened."

Lyle raised his eyebrows. He wasn't so sure Linda was understanding her husband.

Lyle's phone buzzed in his pocket. Since Kylie's day skipping school, he had a tracking app on his phone that went off whenever her phone came in and out of the area. She must be about to come back with her grandfather. He set the phone on the white wooden table as he and Linda continued to chat.

The front door creaked open as Linda was asking about holding a local vigil to raise awareness. Hearing this, Tom started to approach the kitchen.

"Yes, we should definitely do that," Lyle agreed.

"We can invite the local news to cover it too," Tom chimed in, now standing behind Lyle.

Lyle grimaced at the thought of having to speak to the media again.

With the phone face up, a large notification appeared on Lyle's phone. For a moment that felt like a decade, they stared at the phone, then both slowly looked up at each other. Linda's eyes narrowed, trying to piece together something so unbelievable.

"Linda, this is not what it looks like," he said, panicking.

A photo glowed between them. It was the torso of a woman in just a lace red bra. She had a small heart tattooed on her left breast. When Tom saw the look on his wife's face, he peered over to see the phone's image before the phone went dark again.

Tom bellowed, "You! You son of a bitch!"

Linda stood up, grabbed Tom's hand, and they turned to leave. "How could you?" Linda shouted over her shoulder.

"What just happened?" Kylie asked, entering the kitchen holding a pink smoothie in her hand.

Lyle shrugged, grabbed his phone and walked into his bedroom, locking the door behind him. He heard his daughter calling after him but it sounded like it was miles away. Right now, it was just him and this image. He sunk to the floor and unlocked his phone, to look at the image that had appeared—an image that would most likely change the trajectory of his life.

From an unknown number, an image of an unknown woman.

Lyle typed back: **Who the hell is this? Stop messaging me.**

Almost immediately three dots appeared.

Unknown number: **Hello Love.**

Lyle: **Who the hell is this? And why the hell do you keep messaging me?**

No more responses came from the other end.

There was no way out of this for him. He had to go to the police and tell them what was happening. If he hid it, it would make him look guilty. The thought occurred to him that maybe someone was trying to frame him but he was sure the police would find that idea laughable.

* * *

Lyle hated being back in this place but he felt he had no other choice. Someone was stalking him or trying to make it appear that way. At this point, he needed protection for himself but more importantly to make sure his little girl was safe.

"Just take a look at my phone," Lyle begged the officer.

The officer took the phone. Lyle could see her eyes widened and knew that she had gotten to the seductive photo. She placed the phone back down and pushed it towards him. "So, you want us to believe that these photos and messages are being sent unsolicited?"

Lyle put his hand around the back of his neck and squeezed from the frustration. "Yes, Ms. Petrov, that is exactly what I am telling you."

"It's Detective Petrov," she corrected. "What did you think when you got this photo?"

"That everyone would think I'm having an affair and then by default, I must have killed Shelley. It's a fucking classic story, isn't it?!"

Petrov shook her head. "Well, I see you haven't responded very warmly to these texts."

"Yeah, no shit. It's driving me crazy. I need you to do something, Detective. Can you trace where these are coming from?"

"Unfortunately, we can't," she said, looking at him with pity. "We don't have the technology for that here."

"Can you send it out to another location? I need to know where these texts are coming from."

"I'll speak to my boss and see what we can do," she said as she jotted down something in her notebook.

Chapter Twenty-Five

A LOUD POUNDING on the door woke Lyle from his mid-day nap. He jolted up and scrambled toward the door.

"Open up!" shouted someone on the other side of the door as the pounding intensified.

Lyle opened the door to see two unfamiliar officers.

"We have a warrant to search your home."

He let the officers in and sat on his front porch. He envisioned them getting to the walk-in closet, one side full of clothing as if nothing was wrong, the other completely bare. Lyle had never found the words to tell them her things were gone, picturing himself being thrown straight into jail the second he uttered the words. Now he had no choice but to try to explain himself.

Through the open window he could hear them shuffling around inside. Lyle's stomach lurched up into his throat and he heaved repeatedly, though nothing came out.

He sat with trembling hands for what felt like an eternity until the two officers emerged and allowed him to reenter his home. It was hard to process what had just happened—could there be a clue here to help find her? Or just evidence that they could skew to make him look guilty?

* * *

Lyle had asked to meet with Detective Petrov again. He hoped the female officer might be a little more sympathetic, more understanding and less likely to jump to a conclusion.

She pulled out her chair and motioned for him to sit across from her. "So, what's going on?"

"There have been strange things happening." Under the table he was balling and un-balling his fists nervously.

Petrov raised her eyebrows. "Go on…"

"I've had things taken from my home. First it was a photo album Shelley had given to Kylie with photos of the two of them. Then, and this is the most alarming, all her clothing had been removed from her closet. When your officers searched the house, I know you saw it, but I swear, I didn't do that. I didn't toss any of her stuff."

Her look seemed to scream, how stupid do you think I am? "Let me get this straight. Your house was broken into and robbed. You said nothing to the police. Then they search your home and you come crawling back here with a reason that your wife's items were tossed?"

His hands were balled so tightly that his nails dug into his palm. "I know it sounds crazy. I'm going crazy! I don't know what I'm supposed to do."

"Crazy is one way to put it. So, let me ask you this—if we check local cameras, we won't find you loading trash bags of clothes into your car? Or dumping them in nearby dumpsters?"

"Absolutely not! I swear." He scanned her brown eyes to see if he could detect her reaction but it was blank.

The detective tapped her pencil on the table and said nothing. He knew what she was doing. She was waiting for him to say more and trip himself up. Well, he wasn't going to give her that satisfaction. They'd just sit there in silence if that's what she wanted.

"You know this doesn't look good for you, Lyle," she said, finally breaking the silence.

Lyle tossed his hands in the air in frustration. "Can you please talk to some of the neighbors and see if anyone came into my house?"

"Yes, we will investigate and find out if it was you...or not."

He squeezed his fists together so tightly that his knuckles were white as ghosts, then stood up. "Well, thanks a lot for your immense help."

Chapter Twenty-Six

May 2025

IT HAD BEEN seven weeks since he last saw his wife walk out the door. He turned on the TV and flipped to the channel that the press conference would be on. His stomach was clenching like someone had gotten a hold of it and squeezed with all their might.

Off to the side of the screen were his in-laws. The officer introduced them and then stepped aside, letting them have the spotlight.

Linda approached the podium and Tom stood behind her. The paper in her hand trembled. "Hello…" her voice cracked and she paused for a second, most likely trying to compose herself. "I am Linda Schwartz and this is my husband Tom. We are the parents of Shelley Schwartz Lazrin. First, we want to thank the Belmar Police for their continued effort to help find our beloved daughter." She paused to look back at the officers and provided them a sad smile. "As we approach the two month mark, we continue to implore the public to look for her and keep her case in your mind." She held up a picture of Shelley, beaming and beautiful. Linda listed off a series of descriptions of Shelley.

Despite the fact that Lyle knew what she was about to say, he still felt incredibly sorry for her. She was a kind woman and he didn't like to see her suffering.

"If you have any information please contact the police." Again, she stopped, unable to continue.

Tom put a hand on her shoulder and gave a little squeeze, like someone gently squeezing fruit to check for ripeness. It must have been the encouragement she needed because she continued.

"Tom and I, after much consideration, would like to announce that at this time, we would like to withdraw our support for Shelley's husband, Lyle. Recently we have seen information that leads us to believe that their relationship was not what we thought it was. We believe he is having an affair and...now that we know this, let's just say our view of the situation is different. We think he might have some role in the disappearance of our daughter." She swayed like a thin tree during a storm and her husband put his hand on her arm to stabilize her.

"Jesus Christ," Lyle mumbled under his breath. He had tried to reach out to them a dozen times to explain but they were set on their current theory and wanted nothing to do with him.

He knew the effect this would have on everything. The public's rallying cry to put him away would only grow louder and louder. He wouldn't be able to leave the house. Kylie would be bullied at school. Though his job wasn't high on his list of concerns right now, no one would want to ever buy houses from a suspected murderer and how would they survive without any income?

His whole world was falling apart.

Once her parents were done, an officer that he didn't recognize came to the podium. Journalists started lobbing questions at the man like someone outnumbered in a snowball fight. He raised his hand to signal for quiet which they obeyed. He began to point to one journalist at a time.

"Is there evidence that shows if Shelley is alive or dead?"

"No, there is nothing definitive at this time," he said matter of factly.

"The parents believe he had an affair. Do the police?"

"There is evidence that could suggest an affair from both husband and wife, although nothing is proven at this point."

Linda and Tom both whipped their heads to the officer. Shelley's affair must have been news to them.

"Will you be arresting Lyle Lazrin?"

"At this time, we are trying to find Shelley. That is our main focus."

Lyle took note of his non-answer and he could feel his anxiety rising. It was getting hard to breathe. If they arrested him, Kylie would have lost both her parents. Lyle sucked in air, but no matter how hard he tried, he couldn't feel like he was getting any. Dizziness set in and as it increased the room around him seemed to spin chaotically, like a bad ride he couldn't get off of.

The officer held up his hands again, looking both exhausted and annoyed.

"We won't be taking any more questions. If you have any information about the disappearance of Shelley Lazrin..."

"Schwartz," Tom politely interjected.

The officer looked back and nodded. "Shelley Schwartz-Lazrin, please call the Belmar police right away. We welcome any and all tips. Big or small. You may not think it matters but it could be a key to solving this mystery. The Belmar Police are committed to following any, and all, leads so that we can bring Shelley home." He turned to walk away, as journalists continued to shout questions over each other.

Lyle grabbed the remote and turned off the TV. Slamming the remote down, he closed his eyes. He knew they would be coming for him next. The thought was too much, he laid down on the couch as the room continued to spin and passed out.

Chapter Twenty-Seven

LYLE HAD BEEN in the same outfit for three days at this point. Without work, or his wife, or a social life, he just didn't see the point. He sat on his couch in a stained t-shirt with a large bag of chips in his lap. He scrolled through news articles, not even processing what he was seeing—just on mindless autopilot at this point.

Out of the blue, Lyle received a text from his old high school friend. His friend Aaron was the same year as Shelley but one year ahead of Lyle. She had introduced the two teens when Lyle moved to town his junior year—their senior year. He always looked up to Aaron and they quickly became best friends. Though, the years and distance had left them barely in communication for a long while now.

He was asking him to meet up. God, how long had it been? Three...four years at least. Last he heard Aaron had moved away to North Jersey after he got married. They fell out of touch shortly after.

The first thing he thought was if he had the energy to get up, showered, and changed. To add socializing on top of it, seemed a bridge too far to cross. When he declined, he got a message back.

I think we really need to meet. I have something I need to talk to you about that might be helpful for you to know.

This piqued his interest enough to agree. Lyle really hoped it was about Shelley. Any information at this point was welcomed.

Meeting anywhere near his home was not an option, so when Aaron asked him to meet up later that day, the meeting place was set for over an hour away. He opened the doors to the hole in the wall establishment and strolled into a sports bar decked out with Eagles and Phillies posters. It smelled of lingering mold and old beer.

Aaron was huddled in the back corner of the bar in a booth. He wore his baseball hat, trying to hide part of his face. The two men shook hands and Lyle slid into the seat across from him.

"You look like shit," Lyle quipped.

"I was going to say the same to you," he retorted.

"Well, I have some things going on. I'm sure you heard."

Aaron nodded. He was wringing his hands and suddenly Lyle became suspicious. Was this a set up? Had his old friend brought him here, maybe wearing a wire, to catch him in a confession. Shit, why hadn't he thought of that before? He was going to have to be very careful about anything he said, just in case.

"That's why I asked you to meet."

A switch of rage flipped in Lyle. Though this was the exact reason he had driven this far, his anxiety was making him irrational. He was like a ticking time bomb just waiting to be lit and Aaron was holding the match.

"Why?! What the hell? You should have told me that instead of luring me out to the god damn boondocks." He slammed his hand on the wooden table.

"Dude, calm down," Aaron said in a lowered tone, looking around the establishment. "Neither of us wants to be seen here. Just...keep cool."

"Keep cool? Jesus. Just tell me whatever the hell you need to say. I can't believe you made me drive all the way to South Jersey for this."

"I saw the news...about Shelley. First, I'm sorry."

Lyle's angry expression softened just a bit.

"They mentioned an affair."

And just like that, the rage was back. "Yeah, everyone keeps saying that. She wasn't having a god damn affair and neither was I."

Aaron cleared his throat. "She was."

"Aaron, just shut up. You don't even know her now!" Waving his finger he practically hit Aaron's face. His voice was bordering on screaming at this point.

"She was," he repeated. "With my stepbrother."

"Stepbrother? I didn't know you had a brother."

"He graduated before you got there and then took off. He was and is a mess. Randy—"

"Randy?" Lyle attempted to lunge at him, but, over the table, it was hard. The two beers toppled over, soaking both men.

"Hey, knock it off over there," shouted the young waitress. "Any more of that and you'll have to leave."

Both men quickly apologized, realizing they weren't doing a very good job of keeping a low profile. The waitress seemed satisfied with their apology and went back to texting.

"I'm sorry man. Just let me explain."

"You knew someone was screwing my wife and didn't bother to tell me until she's...gone. What is there to explain? I know we haven't talked in a while, but you used to be a good friend."

"It wasn't like that. I don't know maybe it was—I wasn't there."

"So why are you telling me this now, Aaron?"

"Because it wasn't any of my business to tell. But when I heard she was missing...well, I started thinking about some things. And I can't keep this to myself in good conscience." Aaron slightly shook his head and then stared off into the distance.

Lyle glared back at him waiting for him to continue.

"Randy didn't have the best track record with women. Especially when he drank, and he drank a lot. He's had a history of domestic violence. The cops know him well around his town. We just never thought it would escalate. Or maybe we did and we were just in denial. You never think someone you know could...oh, God." Aaron buried his face in his hands.

"You gotta go to the cops with me. You have to tell them this."

Aaron didn't respond.

Lyle lowered his voice and leaned into his former friend. "Aaron, they think she's dead and that I did it. I don't think they've even looked at anyone else. I could go to jail for something I didn't do if you don't help me out. And then our daughter wouldn't have anyone. Can you do that in good conscience? You could help them find her. Remember Shelley, the girl who helped you find a prom date after two girls rejected you? How she introduced us your senior year and we became thick as thieves. Shelley, the woman who sent you meals after your mother passed away even though you hadn't spoken in years."

Aaron closed his eyes, taking in Lyle's words.

When he didn't respond Lyle added, "That's the girl you need to be thinking about right now."

Aaron looked down at his beer, weighing his options.

Aaron could see her image behind his closed eyes. He recalled vividly all those moments Lyle was imploring him to think about, but more importantly he remembered how she made him feel—loved, Shelley made people feel loved.

He lifted his head. A mental image played in his mind—all the life experiences he had with his stepbrother and with his former best friend. How could he interject himself into something that would alter either of their life paths? He thought again of Shelley and her kindness and knew what he had to do.

Aaron picked up his beer and took a long chug, nearly finishing it. "Yeah, okay. Let's go. Let's go talk to the police." He slammed down the beer stein and stood up, Lyle following behind him.

Chapter Twenty-Eight

STANDING OUTSIDE THE POLICE STATION, Lyle waited impatiently. He paced back and forth as he scanned the parking lot. Time kept creeping by and no sight of his former friend.

Lyle frantically dialed Aaron. *Where was this asshole?* he thought to himself. The phone went to voicemail and a curse loudly escaped his mouth.

Just his luck, Detective Petrov walked by as he did so. "Probably not the best idea to come outside the police station and yell curse words into the void."

Lyle explained to her the situation with Aaron but she looked at him skeptically.

"Come on in, you can sit in my office until he gets here."

Lyle followed behind her, wondering if voluntarily entering the station was a good idea. "I'll stay here and wait for him," he said, settling into a plastic seat in the lobby.

"Suit yourself," she replied.

He sat in the waiting area, knee bobbing up and down, while Petrov went off to do her work. Each time the door opened he looked over expectantly.

Lyle's phone buzzed in his pocket. A notification—Shelley was sharing her location with him. His heart stopped and his hand went to his chest. He quickly opened the app and tried to find her, but she wasn't on the screen. It had been disabled again.

Without thinking, he shot up and asked to have Petrov come out to speak with him.

"What's going on?"

"Did you see that?" he said pointing frantically to the phone but it was gone.

Petrov looked confused. "What?"

"Shelley, or someone with her phone, was sharing her location. But it's off again. I only got a notification but before I could open the app it was off again. Can you track that? Can you find out where it was coming from?" His words were tumbling out quickly, bordering on maniacal. He just wanted to find his wife so badly that he could physically feel it clenching every part of himself.

Petrov put her hand on his shoulder and spoke to him in a hushed tone. "I'm afraid we can't. If it came on and off like that, it was probably a glitch. I'm sorry. I know that must be hard to hear."

Lyle's knees buckled and he stumbled back into the chair. He tossed the phone on the small table and left his phone facing up with the app open. His eyes were glued to the screen, hoping he could will it to show him a clue where she might be. "Just tell me...do you think she could still be out there? I need to tell my daughter that her mom is coming home again, that she will be able to have her mother cheer for her at her graduation and help her plan her wedding." Lyle put his hands over his face, creating a mask to the world, and began to bawl. His grief was so strong, he didn't even think to feel embarrassed or ashamed of his tears.

The detective sat in the seat next to him and leaned in a little. She was chewing minty gum that filled the air around him. As she leaned he smelled something else, something familiar nearly masked by the gum. He couldn't place it, but it made him ache for Shelley.

"I can't answer that. But you and your daughter will need to lean on each other no matter what happens. Focus on that bond. Find comfort with each other."

When Lyle composed himself, he looked up at her. "Thank you. You are very kind."

At that moment, the door opened and there was Aaron. He walked in and looked around, seeing Lyle with the officer. For a few seconds, he just stared at them, looking like he'd been hit by a truck. His eyes were bloodshot as if he had been crying.

"Where the hell were you? I've been here for over an hour."

Aaron shrugged. "I just need to talk to the detective alone."

Petrov stood up and motioned for him to follow her back to where Derzo was, leaving Lyle in the waiting area alone again.

Aaron began to tell his story slowly at first but then once he started it was hard to stop the flow of thoughts. He told of his brother's history of domestic violence, what he knew of his relationship with Shelley, and most concerningly, that when he called his brother on the way to the station, he threatened to take his own life.

The two detectives sat in silence the whole time, only the sound of typing into their laptops could be heard in the small room. When he was finally done speaking, Aaron slouched, exhausted from it all.

Derzo looked up from his laptop. "Why did you decide to tell us all this? Why now?"

Aaron sucked in a breath. "Because I've known my stepbrother my whole life, and I've known Lyle for at least a decade. And, it pains me to say this but, I think you are going after the wrong person."

"Don't dance around it. Say what you need to say," Derzo said.

"If Shelley isn't alive—I think...I think Randy is more likely to be involved than Lyle."

The two detectives excused themselves and went to speak privately.

Petrov spoke first. "Wasn't expecting that today."

"What do you make of it?"

"I think it takes a lot of courage to come out against a family member."

"Or a lot of hatred. We need to look into what their relationship is like. He could easily be doing this for revenge or some other motive. For all we know, he was the one actually seeing her."

"True. But I didn't get that impression."

"I agree. He seems believable but regardless we need to dot all our I's and cross our T's."

If there was any truth to Aaron's words, they had been going in the wrong direction for quite some time now. This meant starting at square one.

How do you know if you're going through a marriage slump? Or your partner just isn't that into you anymore? Or that they are just tired? Or apathetic?

The most reasonable thing I could do is ask her... but would she even be honest with me? And if I was way off base, well that would be mortifying.

Things just seem off. Hot and cold. I don't know what to say or do.

* * *

Excerpt from the personal diary of Shelley Lazrin, Dated August 2024

After talking for months and months, I finally met up with Randy today for the first time. There was so much build up- we've been talking constantly lately. Of course, I felt guilty...but also doing something wrong was a little thrilling? It helped mask the pain of losing...

But that didn't last long. There was zero chemistry. We clicked so well online but everything was just off...

It's for the best though. I deleted him from my phone and Facebook- like it never happened. I'm going to get back on track and focus on Lyle and Kylie. And pray Lyle never finds out.

Lyle was called back in after Aaron was done. He sat with the two detectives. "Are you going to look into this Randy guy?" A little flicker of hope lit up through all the darkness. But it was also a crushing feeling. It wasn't a hope that he'd see his wife, just that he might get some answers.

"Of course," said Derzo. "We will explore all leads."

"But what do you think?"

"We can't really go into that with you," said Petrov. "Obviously, we will do everything we can until we find out what happened to Shelley."

"This is all so impossible to comprehend. She's been gone so long. At this point, I'm trying not to lose faith but..."

"What?" Derzo asked.

"It's not likely that she's still with us, right?"

They didn't respond at first.

"There have been all sorts of impossible outcomes with missing person cases. Some people have returned completely fine after decades, just walked away on their own. Some people, even with all the technology today, have been able to reinvent themselves else-where. We really don't know at this point but we want to keep an open mind until we find evidence that leads us in a certain direction."

"Okay, but those types of cases are like a one in a million chance. I doubt she's on the goddamn beach drinking a margarita while we all suffer here."

"We are just saying that we aren't losing hope of finding her and we hope you all will keep the faith too. That's all we can do for now until we know more about the situation."

"In a few days, it will be Mother's Day. And Kylie has no mother, no answers. If she isn't with us, I'd rather know now so I can help my daughter cope."

"You don't mean that," Petrov said softly. "You still have hope she's alive."

Lyle looked her straight in the eye. "For a while I did—but it's been too long. She wouldn't do that to Kylie. She wouldn't let her celebrate Mother's Day wondering, grieving like this." And then he let the words out that he had held on to for so long. He hoped keeping them to himself would mean they weren't true. "I think she's dead. If she's gone, we need to know now. We can't heal until they find her." Lyle looked down, tightly squeezing the bridge of his nose as he heard the two officers exhale.

Chapter Twenty-Nine

LYLE SAT in the car pickup line, flipping through his phone as he waited for his daughter. He knew he shouldn't, but he decided to look through the comments section of articles related to the case. Every single comment was a punch to the gut. Not a single comment was in support of Lyle. How could he possibly continue to live in a town that thought this about him?

Before he went any deeper down the rabbit hole, the car door opened and Kylie plopped into the seat next to him. "How was school, kiddo?"

"Eh," she said as she pulled her phone out of the neon pink backpack.

"Guess that's better than bad, so I'll take it. I noticed you haven't been asking to hang out with friends lately. Do you want to invite a friend over? We can get pizza. They can even sleepover if you want."

Kylie didn't answer.

"Ky?"

She glared at him but his eyes were on the road as he pulled out of the school parking lot. "Dad...people can't come over."

"It's fine. I'd clean up more before they came. Sorry it hasn't been as clean as..." his voice trailed off. There was no need to finish his thought.

"Dad! They aren't allowed over, okay? Can we just drop it?"

"Is that why you didn't want to ride the bus today?"

"I asked you to drop it."

He knew better than to push her when she was in this state so he simply replied, "Sure." It hadn't even occurred to him that parents wouldn't let their kids be around him anymore, and it stung that this was going to just be another thing taken away from Kylie.

He had an idea he had been tossing around but wasn't sure how his pre-teen would react. "So..." he drew out slowly.

"Oh, God, what?"

Already off to a great start he thought. "At least give me a chance to tell you before you write it off."

She shrugged her shoulders.

Lyle kept his eyes on the road as he drove. This way he could avoid any eye rolls or cringes. "I think we should get away for a weekend, doesn't have to be right now...but I think we could use an escape from social media...and this town."

"Yeah, I'd actually really like that. But nowhere that we went as a family please. Someplace new."

Her enthusiasm, or at least the tween version of it, surprised him.

They chatted back and forth about possible options—not too far away so they could drive. Close enough they could get back in time if they were needed for something related to Shelley. But something more remote so they could feel like they were removed from all of this relentless pain. By the time they reached their house, they decided a trip to the Poconos would be a good and quick getaway.

Lyle pulled into the driveway when an idea popped into his head. He turned to his daughter. "Hey—why don't we stop by Thunder Road Books and get a book to read on the trip?"

"Can we stop at Driftwood for a coffee too?"

"Deal," he replied. He pulled out of the driveway and they

continued to chat about the possible trip. It was such a welcome distraction.

They each ordered an iced coffee and took it to go. Lyle smiled at his daughter as they walked out of the coffee shop. Sometimes it was impossible to please her, and other times it just took a cup of joe.

At the little bookstore, they asked the woman behind the counter if she could point them in the direction of popular fiction. Lyle followed behind the woman, not realizing that Kylie wasn't behind him.

"Are you looking for something specific?"

"I'm just looking for a book to read on—on my porch. Thank you," he said with a huge fake smile. Lyle suddenly became nervous. He almost said, 'on my trip.' Should he be telling people he planned to go away? It felt reckless. He trusted no one.

"That sounds nice." She turned to go back to the cash register.

Lyle found the book that interested him and then grabbed a few other random books nearby.

He found his daughter, with a similar stack at her feet. She was in the true crime section, running her fingers along the spines. Lyle cleared his throat so she would know he was there, but giving her time to respond.

She glanced over her shoulder. "What if she ends up in a book here one day? What if people I know come in, buy a book about the abduction of my mother to entertain themselves while they sit on the beach?"

Lyle felt like he had been hit by a wave that knocked him to his knees. "I know this is all so painful and I wish I had the right words to say to you, Kylie."

"You don't have to. Sorry, I shouldn't have come to this section. I knew it would hurt."

He put the books on the ground and met her gaze. "You have nothing to apologize for."

Lyle saw the pain in her face and she quickly changed the topic. "Can I get these?" And she pointed to a stack of seven books.

At that point she could have asked for a pet tiger and he would have said yes. "Absolutely. Let's go check out." He peered over at the stack, surprised she had moved on from the tween drama books to a fantasy series. He knew the escape of wandering through moonlit forests and soaring through the air on the back of a dragon would be just what she needed.

When they arrived home, Kylie put her stack of books on her desk. Then she returned to the living room and sat with her father as they searched for a cabin in the mountains. Together the pair talked about meals they could make and what board games to bring. They looked for nearby hikes—short and moderate. It was a moment that they could finally breathe and bond like they had before all this happened.

As his daughter opened an app to write out their grocery list, Lyle worried that the police might not take his travel too well. He knew he would have to inform them and it pissed him off that 'innocent until proven guilty' doesn't seem to apply when your wife goes missing. He felt like a criminal having to report his comings and goings.

"Can we get stuff to make s'mores?"

Lyle pulled back into reality, realizing that his thoughts were tumbling so quickly that he hadn't even processed what his daughter was saying.

"Dad! I said, can we make s'mores?" she snapped, a bit annoyed.

"Yeah, yeah, of course. Sorry. I was thinking about...work."

She rolled her eyes. "Yeah okay...You better pay attention or you might end up agreeing to something crazy like buying me beer! And then mom would be really pissed at you!" She smiled at her joke for the slightest of seconds and then it hit her. There was no mom right now. No one to reprimand poor decisions. No one to guide her in the right direction. The smile slipped from her face slowly, like an ice cream cone melting on a hot day, as her eyes grew wider in dismay at her own foolish comment.

"It's okay, Ky..." and he pulled her into a hug. Her small body quivered in his arms, slightly at first but growing in intensity. Before he could realize it, he was crying too. "It's okay, Ky," he repeated. "It's going to be okay." Though he didn't believe that.

Chapter Thirty

THOUGH IT WAS A SCHOOL DAY, they both woke up late as Lyle had intentionally turned off all the alarm clocks the night before. They just needed to work on their own schedule for right now. Trying to maintain normalcy at this time just wasn't always possible and frankly it wasn't good for their mental health, he reasoned.

After dropping her off at school two hours late, Lyle went home. Normally he'd be working with clients but given the situation, his prospects had dried up. Lyle began to flip through his phone, mindlessly searching Reddit to see if his wife's case was mentioned in any of the true crime sub reddits. He knew that no good would come from this but he was a glutton for punishment.

There was a post: Belmar Mother Goes Missing. The original poster kept to the facts without much speculation. However, things devolved rapidly in the comments. He could feel chills running down his spine when he read the comment:

I wonder if we can figure out where this guy lives.

And the response below it:

Yeah, someone needs to get the daughter OUT of that house before he hurts her too!

People felt emboldened to say whatever they wanted on the internet...but what if some of them followed through? The idea of some vigilante trying to take Kylie away was terrifying.

Lyle quickly dialed the police station and asked to speak to Derzo.

"Detective Petrov."

"Oh, hi. I had asked to speak to Derzo."

"Sorry, he isn't here now. Guess you'll just have to speak to me."

Lyle filled her in on the situation and tried to gauge her thoughts on whether or not Kylie was in any real danger.

Petrov listened and when he finally stopped speaking she reassured him that things would be okay. "You know how people on the internet can be, everyone feels like they can say anything—things they would never dream of in real life. Do you know what I mean?"

Lyle sighed heavily. "Okay, yeah, I guess you are right, but I'm still very nervous."

"I don't want your daughter to feel worried. I can request a patrol officer drive by throughout the evening."

"Yes, that would be helpful. Thanks for your assistance, Detective. I really appreciate you taking the time to help me through this."

On the other end, Petrov gave a weak smile. "Anytime Mr. Lazrin."

"Lyle, call me Lyle."

She cleared her throat. "Anytime Lyle," she said softly.

"Hey, um, would it be okay if Kylie and I went away for a long weekend? Some place close?"

She shrugged. "I don't see any issue with it."

She had helped calm his nerves a bit but he couldn't resist continuing to read each and every comment. It was like a vortex that was pulling him under, continuing with the obsessive doom scrolling. While he was searching, a text came up, again from an unknown number. He braced himself for whatever would be on the screen.

There was a cropped photo of a woman. She was tugging on her shirt, exposing the top part of her chest which was covered by the same red lacy bra. Right above the lace line was a tattoo, a small heart now with an L in the middle. The text below it read: **For you, my Love.**

He dropped the phone to the floor and it fell face up. Lyle propped himself so he just stared at the image until the screen faded into darkness.

Chapter Thirty-One

Mother's Day, 2025

THE WINTER HAD RESCINDED, and signs of spring were gently making themselves known. The days grew longer, the air was brisk but no longer chilly. A few small flowers poked through the ground, adding little bursts of color here and there.

As Lyle sat on the porch swing, he heard birds chirping for the first time in months. Normally, this was a sign a real estate agent looked forward to as it coincided with an increase in sales. Unfortunately, he was still finding it impossible to gain clients.

Though the world around him was bursting with color, Lyle felt empty and cold. Two more days would mark two full months of her disappearance. It always hurt, but today was unbearable- like every part of him was constricting.

His daughter had asked to be left alone today, so she was in her room, pretending it was any other day. With a book in hand, he tried to read but couldn't focus. His eyes moved over the words but he wasn't able to pull any meaning out of them. He wondered where his wife was physically and where his daughter was mentally. The thought caused him to flip open the tracking app.

It has been days since Lyle stopped checking his wife's location every few seconds. He had now gotten down to checking a few times an hour. Despite the fact that he got notifications from the app, it was a compulsion at this point. He gazed at the screen mindlessly. A surge of panic arose in Lyle when he, yet again, got a notification that Shelley had started sharing her location. A little blue circle appeared with an S, indicating that she was only blocks away. He prayed it wasn't another glitch.

"Kylie! I'm going out," he called down the hallway.

She realized there was panic in his voice and emerged from her room to assess the situation. Lyle was so focused on this moment that he didn't realize his daughter had started running behind him.

A surge of energy he had never felt before propelled him to his destination. His heart was pounding through his shirt. Lyle kept his eyes locked on the screen, watching his bubble grow closer to hers with each step.

He sprinted the two blocks to the beach. He had envisioned this moment of reconnection many times. Sometimes there was anger, sometimes a barrage of questions. But as the moment drew towards the real possibility of seeing her again, he knew all he would do was hold her.

The cool winds by the coastline made the beach nearly empty. He climbed the few stairs up to the boardwalk and then the few stairs down to the beach. With such focus, he didn't hear the footsteps tracking directly behind him.

It wasn't until he stopped that he could feel how much the long run had taken out of him and he began to breathe heavily. There was a thick fog hovering over the sand like a winter blanket and it made it difficult to see. He scanned the beach as best he could, moving through the low clouds.

And there she was.

"Shelley!" His voiced ripped through the quiet. His wife lay face down in the sand, arm outstretched, a large sunhat covering her head. Her cellphone laid tossed beside her.

"Mom!!!!!" The sound that came from his daughter was like her heart was leaving her body with the words. She crumbled to her knees and he was torn between going to Kylie and going to Shelley.

"Turn around," he commanded. He approached his wife and lifted the sun hat. He put his hand to her neck to check for a pulse, but there was none. She was ice cold to the touch. His mind wouldn't let him understand the situation, so he placed his hand on her back to check for breathing. He called to her over and over as if he could just wake her from a deep sleep.

Kylie at this point had turned around. "Mommy!" Her voice cracked. Kylie walked closer to her father and whispered, "No, no, no. She's gone, Dad."

He couldn't respond to those words. The anguish overtook him and he screamed until it hurt. He crawled over to be closer to his daughter. They lay on the ground crying, enveloped in the fog like the hug they so desperately needed. Sadness and confusion swirling to make an unbearable cocktail.

Lyle thought how this would be their last time together as a family of three. How this memory would creep into all other memories of her, like invasive vines. It sickened him. He quickly pulled away from his daughter and heaved until there was nothing left in his stomach. When he was done, she reached for her father again, ignoring the foul odor in the air.

As they lay in each other's arms, several passersby heard the commotion and called the police. Police and EMT sirens could be heard getting increasingly louder. Lyle didn't want them to come and see his wife lying there like this. They'd fruitlessly take her pulse and check for breathing, as he had, slowly shaking their heads to say she was gone. They'd put a white sheet over her, a signal to the world that this light had been put out. They'd put her on a stretcher and in the ambulance as just another patient in their day's work.

That would be the end. They'd be a family without a mother. He would be a husband without a wife.

All the anger he harbored toward his wife disappeared like a cloud of smoke and he just ached for her and the future they should have had. The moments he could have said I'm sorry, you were always enough.

Chapter Thirty-Two

"SIT DOWN, Mr. Lazrin. First, I'd like to say I'm sorry for your loss," said Derzo sympathetically, but Lyle felt nothing, knowing he must have uttered this phrase so many times in his career. He was just doing his job.

Lyle didn't respond. He felt like a shell of himself. As if his whole personality had been sucked from him and he was just a walking, breathing corpse.

"We have a few questions for you. I know this is difficult but we need this information to try to find out what happened. We'd like to review your cell phone again."

Lyle didn't respond but tossed the phone in their direction.

Derzo made a grimace, like he was trying to hold back his anger. Again, he continued, "I'm going to step out and give you a few minutes to process this all and maybe calm down a bit. When I come back, I will need you to cooperate. If we have any hope of solving this, we need you to tell us any helpful information."

Lyle just lifted his eyebrows in response. No amount of time would heal this pain.

. . .

Derzo grabbed Lyle's phone and walked out of the room. Lyle stared at the wall. He barely moved when the door opened again. Petrov walked in and sat down across from him. She rubbed on her chest as she sat down. He could feel her watching him.

Derzo returned shortly after.

Her partner looked over at her as she continued rubbing her chest.

"You okay?"

She laughed sheepishly. "Yeah. I definitely ate something that didn't agree with me. Guess I'm getting old—greasy food is giving me heartburn."

Derzo smiled at her. "If you are old what does that make me?"

"An ancient relic," she joked.

Lyle looked at them dumbfounded. He couldn't believe they were just having a normal conversation in the middle of the most horrific moment of his life. Is this what grief would always be like? Like you are on the other side of life, just watching it go by as if it was a movie?

He paused before responding, knowing he would say something really out of line. He counted to three then said, "I'm sorry to interrupt your conversation but can we please focus on Shelley?"

Derzo looked a bit embarrassed. "Yeah, sorry. Sorry. I actually left my files on my desk. I'll be right back." And he stood to leave the room, closing the door behind him.

Petrov watched him and Lyle looked away uncomfortably. When he looked back, she was still staring at him, twirling a strand of her bright red hair. "Meow," she said, smiling devilishly.

Lyle furrowed his brow, causing deep wrinkles to appear.

Before he could respond, the door opened again.

"Petrov, the recording system in here stopped working. We have to move to another room." His voice had a touch of panic.

"Oh no!" she said, and winked at Lyle.

He slowly got up and followed behind her, keeping his eyes glued to her.

. . .

When they got to the new room, everything seemed normal again. Lyle decided that he had completely imagined the whole experience. His mind was going into overdrive because of what he had seen. It was ripping away the few strands of sanity that he had left. That was the only logical explanation.

Lyle told himself to focus. He needed to stop letting his mind play tricks on him. Lyle loosened his tense muscles and pushed all other thoughts out of his mind. He locked eyes on the two officers in front of him, eager to help in any way he could to bring justice to Shelley's case, and hopefully closure for their now smaller family.

Chapter Thirty-Three

Two days after the discovery of Shelley's body...

LYLE ENTERED THE TEMPLE, a place he rarely went with his wife. He was unsure of who would even want him to approach them so he stood in the lobby awkwardly waiting for anyone to come to him, his hands in constant motion, unsure where to land.

Shelley's older brother, Joshua, came up. His tone and his glare were icy. "You need to put on a kippah." And he tossed one at Lyle and then walked off.

Despite only having been found two days ago, the synagogue was filled. The people who loved her dropped everything to attend the service. Some people traveled from across the country. As he scanned the crowd, he knew it was a visual of the impact she made.

Lyle and Kylie made their way to the front, sitting in a pew separated from his in-laws. He ran his hands over the red fabric, so he could feel anything in that moment, something to ground and focus him before his mind spiraled away from him.

. . .

After her parents spoke, Lyle approached the bema. "I want to thank you all for coming here today to honor the life of my wife, and mother to our daughter Kylie. What can I say about Shelley that you don't already know? Well, probably a lot actually." There was some awkward laughter. Some people in the audience looked sideways to gauge other's reactions.

"Shelley was caught in the balance of everything she did. Everything was too much and never enough. She would emanate light and then suck it all out of the room. But through her ups and downs, she was always, always an amazing mother. Which is evident in the strong, kind daughter we see before us." He lovingly smiled at his daughter and her lips ever so slightly tilted up, not able to fully smile back.

"Some may be thinking right now—how could he say such things about someone no longer with us? Who among us isn't caught in the balance of life? Who among us isn't satisfied but also craving more? And like each of us, Shelley did the very best she could given the pressures of it all."

In the crowd Tessa raised her eyebrows in dismay. She leaned over and whispered to her husband and he shrugged his shoulders. Tessa shook her head and wore a scowl. She was now annoyed with both Lyle and her husband.

"I know what many of you think about me, about what happened to my wife. And you know what—you are right."

. . .

People shifted in their seats uncomfortably. Lyle's in-laws turned their heads quickly to face each other, shock taking over their faces.

"In some ways, I feel responsible for everything that happened. Did I care for her enough when she needed me? No. I was selfish and just wanted her to snap out of her low moods, just be happy, enjoy the life she had. Well, I didn't realize until it was too late, that wasn't even possible. So instead of using the time I had with her to support her, understand her, make her feel seen, I pushed her away. And now I'll never get the chance to pull her back in and tell her that I loved her with every ounce of my being. So, if I may ask of you one thing, don't make the mistake I did. I will always be a prisoner of my own guilt."

In the audience Tessa scoffed again and many people looked over her way. Her husband sunk down in his seat.

"Don't get caught up in how everything should be or could be and appreciate what you have in that moment. That moment is all you have—and hopefully it won't be your last like it was mine." Lyle's voice cracked at the end and he held up a hand asking for a moment. A thick hard lump formed in his throat. His regret was choking him. The temple was silent, waiting for him to continue.

"But today isn't about my regrets. Maybe some of you here have something you regret too. But I beg you not to let that bog you down but to use this as a time to reflect on how to be better with those you love.

. . .

"See, death is final for the person who passed through our lives, but she lives on in all of us. We are all here today because Shelley touched us in some way. When she left this Earth, all her memories stayed with us and will always be with us. The moments you had with Shelley transformed you in some way and, though she is gone, who you are and who she was are braided together, because of her time with you, she will always remain, and that is how she is with us eternally."

"Thank you." Lyle said quietly and stepped down off the stage. He went to his seat and sat close to his daughter. He was too taken with the moment to notice that most people had tears in their eyes or that couples reached for their partner's hand and glanced at each other, showing appreciation that they still had their loved one.

Right after the ceremony ended, Linda broke away from Tom and approached Lyle. "Thank you, Lyle, for your kind words about Shelley." She saw Tom coming towards them and excused herself quickly, returning to her husband's side.

After the service was over, the mourners awkwardly greeted Lyle and thanked him for his speech, for his compassion in remembering someone they held in their hearts.

They weren't sure if he was a grieving husband or the cause of her death.

People didn't know how to act around him and he could sense that. As Lyle talked with someone Shelley knew from elementary school, who he had never met, he saw Tessa dragging her husband out of the sanctuary.

The funeral was today. It's real now. It's final.

I said it at the funeral and it's true- I am locked in a cage with my own guilt. The key thrown away with her last breath.

Everything I did wrong- all the times that I didn't respond to her pain, too busy with my own life. I left her there suffering alone- how could that have not made her pain worse? The one person she was supposed to depend on, and I left her alone to wallow in grief.

She had dreams I never supported. What could she have accomplished? I'll always wonder that.

I also said at the funeral that I felt like I killed her, and I did. I killed her spirit with all my mistakes.

Chapter Thirty-Four

THE FOLLOWING WEEK, Lyle's phone rang and he was surprised to see Tessa's number.

"Yeah?" he answered curtly.

"Hello to you too, Lyle."

"I really have nothing to say to you," he replied dryly.

"Well, I think you are going to want to hear this."

"Tessa, I don't have time for games. Just tell me what you are calling for."

"Randy. They found him dead last night."

"Shit." Lyle felt goosebumps prickling his arms and a shiver ran down his back. If he had anything to do with it, there would never be justice for Shelley. "What happened?" he asked.

"Seems like he jumped off the bridge between Belmar and Neptune. But who knows—maybe that isn't the case," she said cryptically. "Lyle, where were you last night?"

"I'm sorry...what?! Tessa, you aren't the goddamn police. What game are you playing?" He muttered under his breath, "Psycho."

She raised her voice. "I need you to tell me where you were last night."

"Tessa, we just had the funeral. Kylie and I were home the whole night. We haven't left the house since the funeral. Kylie said we need to sit sheeva."

"Jesus Christ. It's SHIVA. Even I know that. And that's a shitty alibi. Home. With a family member. Worst alibi and everyone knows that."

"Is it? You've watched some true crime and now you think you're the damn police. I'm sure you of all people know the neighbors have doorbell cameras, right Tessa? If I left, they'd have evidence of that. I gotta go. If you want to do any more detective work, call Petrov and Derzo. I really gotta go."

"Wait! I spoke with Petrov this morning."

"Okay..."

"What do you think of her?"

"She's fine. They are both fine." Though she couldn't see it, he rolled his eyes, becoming increasingly annoyed with this conversation. He was completely done talking to her and couldn't get off the phone fast enough.

"Do you think she's a bit...I don't know...odd?"

Lyle thought for a moment. He wasn't sure if Tessa was trying to set him up. He'd go with a non-answer and feel out the situation. "What makes you ask that?"

"Lyle, I went to talk to her about Randy...and she kept asking about you."

"Yeah, of course. As you know from your podcasts and YouTube videos—being her husband and all, I'm pretty much the prime suspect." Lyle kept checking his watch, eager to get off the phone.

"It wasn't like that, Lyle. Listen to me, she was asking very strange questions about you and Shelley. Like, some of them were really...like, inappropriate."

"Yeah, she's done things like that with me recently. It's all just these shitty head games." Lyle puffed out a big sigh, eager to get off the phone.

"Lyle, I'm telling you, that is NOT what this was. She asked if I knew how often you two slept together."

Lyle paused. "Yeah, she wants to see if we had a good relationship. I'm done with this conversation."

"Fine. Just keep more vigilant, okay? Promise me for Kylie's sake. I might talk to Derzo about it."

Lyle shook his head. "Don't you dare! Stop meddling in this, Tessa. Seriously, stay the hell out of it all. You aren't helping. Like I said, I gotta go." And without waiting for a goodbye on the other end, he disconnected the call.

Lyle sat on the bench between 11th and 12th Ave, his elbows propped on his knees. A pudgy man approached and sat next to him. He was visibly nervous and it made Lyle uncomfortable so he slid down the bench just a bit more.

"Good seeing you again. Thanks for meeting me here," he said without looking at Lyle.

Lyle shook his head, unsure how to respond to that. The last time he saw him was at the funeral.

Earlier in the day, Lyle had received a call from the man wanting to discuss Shelley's disappearance with him. He wasn't sure if it would be anything valuable but at this point, he was grasping at straws. He'd take any information he could get.

"Listen, you can't tell anyone that this information came from me."

Lyle knew he'd do with the information whatever he needed to but he agreed anyway. "Yeah, absolutely." Lyle let the silence hang between them, waiting for the man to share when he was ready.

The man took a deep breath and then finally began to speak. "She's gonna kill me if she finds out," he said, shaking his head with a defeated chuckle. He said no more so Lyle tried to encourage him by ensuring him it would all be okay.

"Well, this case, Shelley's murder, has taken over my wife's life. And, I guess, in some ways I can understand that. Shelley was her best friend. But Tessa just seems so hyper obsessed with it. You'd expect that she'd be worried and maybe proactive about it but she's angry like I've never seen her before."

Lyle nodded his head trying to show he was actively listening but he wasn't sure what this man's point was. He was no fan of her but he didn't hear anything in this confession that stood out to him as being worrisome.

The man reached down into the reusable shopping bag he had and pulled out a small red velvet box. He opened it exposing two rings. Lyle's stomach seemed to lurch into his throat. It was Shelley's engagement and wedding ring set.

"Why do you have that?!" Lyle demanded.

The man became defensive. "It's not mine! That's why I asked to meet you here. I found this in Tessa's nightstand and I didn't recognize it. With her strange behavior, I just wanted to ask you if it was connected to Shelley in any way. Clearly, by your facial expression, it is."

"Did you ask her about it? Like, how she got it? Why she has it?"

The man just laughed softly in response. This man was irritating the hell out of Lyle but he was also thankful that he gave him this information.

"I appreciate you meeting me here and all but what the hell is funny about this?"

"Sorry. It's just the idea of confronting Tessa. But I'm here now, okay?"

"So why do you think she has these? How did she get them?"

The man looked off down the boardwalk for a second before responding. "I think she took them but I'm not sure how, or why. Obviously, you keep that and I'll just get a similar box to put back in the spot. Pray for me she doesn't notice."

Lyle had to ask. "Are you afraid of her?"

The man shook his head. "No, it's not like that. It's just, if you cross her, she goes crazy. I just don't have the energy to deal with it. So, I keep on her good side as much as possible." His shoulders hunched at the admission, making him grow smaller.

Lyle slipped the box into the pocket of his shirt. "Thanks again for meeting with me," he said.

He stood to get up and the man grabbed his arm. "Remember, you can't tell anyone we met." There was real fear in the man's eyes and Lyle felt sorry for him.

"Yeah, I mean what can I do? I've got the ring here. What can I even tell the police?" Before he had uttered those words, Lyle had every intention of going to the police with this fact but now realized that wasn't even possible. They would both deny it and it would look like he was just making up evidence. Another dead end.

Lyle was just hitting roadblock after roadblock.

Chapter Thirty-Five

DESPITE HIS APPREHENSION about being seen in public around town, they were out of food so a trip to the grocery store was needed. As he walked down the aisles with Kylie's list, Lyle saw Tessa pushing her cart. He picked up his pace, unsure what he would even say to her. "Hi Tessa," he said from behind her.

She jumped. "Shit, Lyle. Don't scare me like that." She said nothing else but her face said, *'What do you want?'*

"I need to talk to you about something." Lyle was making up the plan as he went.

"I thought you didn't want to talk to me," she retorted.

He ignored her. "During the event with the flyers, I'm not sure you know this but I had cameras inside the house too. Just for protection." He let his words just hang there, so she could come to her own conclusions and sweat a bit.

"As you know, sometimes people who are guilty will come to these events so the police put up cameras around the place. If they did show up, we'd have them on film. The police reviewed all the footage." He was testing her to see if she'd crack. He wasn't even sure what he was saying made sense. Lyle didn't have much of a choice at this point so he kept the charade going.

Tessa began shifting her weight from one foot to another the more he spoke. "Okay, what's your point?"

Lyle leaned in and lowered his voice, a whispering growl. "I saw what you took."

Tessa raised her hand and Lyle caught it before she could make contact with his face.

"Violence is never the answer, Tessa. Tell me why you took it."

Tessa's eyes narrowed and he could feel her hatred for him radiating off of her. "I'm not telling you anything."

"Tell me or I'll go to the cops," he bluffed.

"Screw you, Lyle. I was worried you would have gotten rid of it and I wanted to make sure it went to Kylie when she turned eighteen, you bastard. I know you had some part in her death. Now, my only goal is to get justice for Shelley and make sure Kylie has the best chance possible at a normal life."

"Come on, Tessa. That still doesn't make sense to me. I think you are hiding something."

"This may be hard for you to understand, but Shelley was my best friend. All I have left to honor her is Kylie. So, I am going to do everything possible to make sure she has a good life."

"Tessa." He leaned in again as people passed. "I mean this in the best way possible—you are a god damn lunatic. You aren't helping the case at all with your stupid stunts. They make you look guilty as hell." Tessa turned on her heels and walked away, leaving her full cart in the aisle. "The truth will come out, Tessa!" he called after her and a woman pushing her cart picked up her pace to a near jog.

Lyle stood there surrounded by brightly colored cereal boxes. He couldn't figure out what was going on with Tessa. She had been interjecting herself into the case in the most bizarre ways possible. She had accused him of hurting Shelley but also fed him information. Nothing about her actions made sense.

Lyle knew he needed to figure out who might be able to shed some light on their friendship. Maybe someone on the PTA saw their dynamic in a different light.

When he got to his car, he opened Facebook and searched through his wife's friend list, looking for anyone who might have a link between Shelley and Tessa. He found a petite blonde woman whose name he recognized, Liza. It was a bold move, but he didn't have many other options at this point.

Hey, Liza, this is Shelley Lazrin's husband. I'd like to meet with you to discuss Shelley. Any information you might have could be helpful—to find justice for Shelley. He waited, tapping the steering wheel for several minutes before getting a response.

Hi, Lyle. I'm so sorry about Shelley. We are all very upset and if I had any useful information I'd gladly help. But I only knew her from a few PTA events so I don't think I can give any new info.

Thanks for getting back to me... It's more about her dynamic with Tessa.

This time the response was swift. **Now that, I have information on.**

The next day Lyle walked into the small coffee shop in Spring Lake. The blonde woman was tucked away in the back, to give them more privacy. Lyle dropped into the seat across from her as she sipped coffee from a mug that said, 'Mondays suck'.

"Thanks for meeting with me, Liza."

"I know what everyone says about you—but I don't think you had anything to do with it."

"Well, thank you. Listen, your time is valuable so I'll just jump into it. What can you tell me about the dynamic between my wife and Tessa."

Liza set her mug down. "When they were together, they worked well. A good team. They got along. Everyone on the PTA liked when they were at events because they got stuff done."

"Yeah, Shelley definitely had a knack for planning events," he said with a small smile.

Liza nodded in agreement and then continued. "But...Tessa wasn't always nice when Shelley wasn't there. It wasn't anything crazy but she'd put her down in this kinda off handed way. And, I'll just say it, we all gossip about each other to some extent. Ya know? But Tessa took it to another level—like, she was trying to turn us against Shelley. So, all of us kinda thought Tessa was just jealous of Shelley and none of us trusted her. Like, who talks about their best friend like that?" Liza lowered her head.

"Do you remember the Saint Patrick's Day dance that Shelley led last year?"

Lyle nodded. "She had green glitter in her hair for a week." And they both gave the smallest smile.

"Well," Liza paused. "Kids who didn't pre-register paid at the door. And some money went missing. Like $150. Shelley was convinced it was Tessa. She told me in confidence. Honestly, I don't know how she handled it. She just told me not to tell anyone else and that she was going to make it right before she had to hand the money over to the treasurer. Tessa put her in a bad spot. I really feel bad for what happened." Liza turned her head to look out the window, hoping to keep the tears from flowing.

"I know this is hard," Lyle said softly.

"I just wish I had told Shelley what Tessa was saying. She deserved a better friend." Liza bit her lower lip and the tears began to trickle down her cheeks. Lyle handed her a napkin and she repeatedly dabbed the corners of her eyes.

Having someone you knew leave this Earth, and in such a violent way, makes you reconsider your own life, your own safety. It was jarring. "You didn't do anything wrong. You couldn't have known what was going to happen," he reassured her and he reached over and patted her hand.

At that moment, as his hand laid on hers, Detective Petrov walked in and her eyes widened at the sight.

A trail of expletives rattled around in Lyle's mind. He quickly excused himself and approached the woman. "Detective, it's not what it looks like."

"Lyle, we can't speak about this here. If you have anything you need to say, it needs to be at the station."

Lyle was so flustered he didn't even say goodbye to Liza. He got into his car and drove towards the station to wait for Petrov.

As he drove, Lyle passed the billboard that had his face plastered on it. From a mile away, he could see that it had been splashed with red paint completely covering his face. It looked like drops of blood dripping down the sign. He gripped the wheel more tightly and continued on.

He spotted her walking in, coffee cup in hand, fifteen minutes later. With her in sight, he bolted out of the car and followed her into the station like a puppy dog. "Can we speak now?"

She whipped around on her heels. "Lyle, you aren't the only case I am working on. Sit down in the lobby and I'll get to you when I get to you." Her normally soft demeanor had flipped and her tone was harsh.

Lyle sat in the waiting area, frequently checking his watch. It was three hours before she came back to retrieve him. He followed behind her. She flung open a door to a small room, where they sat across from each other.

"I know this doesn't look good," he started and she scoffed. "Please, just hear me out before you make a judgement. I was meeting Liza to talk to her about Tessa. There is nothing going on between us. Anyway, a lot of interesting information has come to light recently."

Petrov cocked her head to the side and raised her eyebrows. She wasn't buying it.

"So, are you a detective now too? I didn't realize they added you to the payroll. Lyle, you need to stay out of this case. It isn't for you to investigate. Let us do our job and we will get to the bottom of it."

"Can I please just tell you what I learned?" His voice was on the verge of begging.

"You're free to spout off whatever you want but I wouldn't recommend it." She leaned in so she was inches from his face and he inhaled her vanilla perfume. He squirmed in his seat. "You really need to think about how your words and actions are making you look right now. People seeing you holding hands with another woman isn't a good look to say the least."

Lyle pulled back. "I wasn't holding her hand! I was comforting her. You have to believe me, Trina."

She threw up her hands in exasperation. "It's Detective Petrov. Only you get to decide how you behave during this time period—but everyone else gets to decide how they interpret that behavior. And you sure as shit look guilty when you do things like that. Are we done here?"

Lyle shrugged and then got up to leave. Petrov pulled out her phone and stared at the cracked screen, a signal that she was done with this conversation. "Please, just talk to Tessa's husband and Liza...shit, I forgot her last name. Started with an M."

She didn't look up from the phone. "Sure, Detective Lazrin. Great work," she responded mockingly.

Lyle was fuming as he got in his car. His fingers curled around the steering wheel and he squeezed until it hurt. He couldn't believe that they wouldn't look into this new information and that they were so dismissive.

I haven't slept in days. We are missing about $150 from the event last week. Tessa played it off like we must have recorded it wrong and that's why the money was off. But she was alone with the cash when I went to the bathroom. So I was trying to figure out how I am going to afford to pay back the funds… then I decided to call Tessa's husband. I told him what happened, and right away he sent me the $150. I feel like a shitty friend but what could I do…

Chapter Thirty-Six

ANOTHER DAY, another trip to the police station. Earlier in the day they had told him he needed to come down to the station. Lyle thought he should just set up his own little room with the amount of time he had to spend here. He sat across from the officers with his coffee cup. He took a long swig, hoping to revive himself a little. It was so bitter he winced. Was it the coffee or did everything feel and taste bitter now?

Derzo tapped the table with his pen. "Lyle, we know you were having an affair."

Lyle nearly choked on the coffee at the mention of it. "A what?!" he shouted.

"You heard me. We've analyzed your phone and have all the data. So, you might as well come clean. It's not like you are even trying to hide it at this point! You're holding hands with another woman already. Your wife's items are cleared out of your house. It's time to come clean."

Petrov leaned in. "Yes, tell us about it, Lyle. It's better for you to be honest and tell us now. It will all come out either way."

She smiled at him...was it seductively? Lyle looked at her and shook his head.

"We have text messages between you and another woman."

"Okay, the only other women I talk to regularly are my mother and my daughter. Occasionally my mother-in-law. I did tell you I was getting strange texts and if you recall—you wouldn't look into it."

"Who is Kat?"

"I'm sorry, what?" Lyle had no idea what they were talking about. Was there ever anyone he had put into his phone with that name? He knew the newer phones just transferred phone numbers with each upgrade…had there been a Kat from way back when? Could it have been the name he entered for a pet sitter? Or someone he had shown a house to? He was completely drawing a blank.

Derzo put Lyle's phone on the table so it lay between them. Lyle grabbed the phone and scrolled through, shocked at what he saw.

"Take a look for yourself," Derzo practically shouted.

His mouth dropped open. The messages he had deleted from the unknown numbers were there—and it showed him responding to them—eagerly. What was happening?

Derzo snatched the phone back from Lyle and began reading aloud.

"I miss you and want you."

"Just give it a month or two and we can be together."

"I love you."

"You've had this phone in your possession. I've had to use a shitty flip phone since you took this. How do I know you didn't put this on there yourselves?" Lyle's words were fire.

Derzo put the phone down with a scowl. He looked at Lyle like he was scum of the Earth. They held each other's gaze, each waiting for the other to break and speak first. "That would be unethical. I don't like you insinuating that. It doesn't look like you are the grieving husband that you've been trying to paint yourself as. And if you are lying about this, you're probably lying about everything else."

"I'm telling you—I didn't send those messages. I think you must have put them on the phone. You know what, let's call the damn number."

Derzo let out a puff of exasperation. "We already did. We called earlier today. Right after that, the number was disconnected. It appears to be a burner phone, which was purchased with your credit card."

"With my card?" he said, shocked. "There is no way!" Lyle reached into his back pocket and took out his worn leather wallet. He flipped through the few cards he had, two Visas, one Mastercard, but the Amex was gone. "Son of a bitch!" He looked up at the officers. "I'm missing a credit card."

The detective smiled at him. "Hmmmm mmm. Sure, you are," he said.

"Interesting how you just realized that now," Petrov chimed in. She looked so smug.

In this moment, Lyle loathed these two with a hatred he had never felt before. His wife was gone and he had no one helping to find the truth. Her murder would go unsolved, eating away at him for the rest of his life. And likely they'd be able to pin it on him, taking his freedom and Kylie's only living parent away from her. He wanted to punch them both.

Derzo's walkie-talkie buzzed static and then a voice came over asking for him. "Yeah, I'm kinda busy now."

"Yeah, we are going to need you to get down here right now. It's regarding the Lazrin case and it's urgent."

Derzo glanced over at Petrov and she shrugged.

"What the hell is going on?"

"Some of the items are missing."

The detective turned off the walkie-talkie and slammed it on to the table. "What the actual fuck is happening around here?" He stormed out of the room.

Lyle wanted to follow him. He did not want to be left alone with Petrov.

She twirled her red hair around her finger. "Hmm, that's weird." And she smiled at Lyle.

"Am I free to sit in the waiting room?" he asked.

"I'd prefer it if you stayed right here so I can keep an eye on you. You don't seem like someone who can be trusted."

Lyle crossed his arms and looked down at the floor, tracing the lines of the tile with his eyes to pass the time and avoid her gaze. A chime went off and Lyle looked up. Her phone on the table was still black. "What was that sound?"

"My phone."

"No, it wasn't. It's off."

She lowered her head. "Yes, it was."

"So, you have more than one phone?"

"Yes, a work phone and a personal phone. Pretty common practice."

When Derzo entered the room again, he was still angry. He tossed a file onto the table between them and it landed with a thud. They kept him there for another few hours, neither party swaying on their original position.

Chapter Thirty-Seven

LYLE STOOD in the brightly colored office with the principal and guidance counselor. The principal pulled out a chair and motioned for Lyle to sit down.

"Thank you for coming in today. I know we've talked before over the phone, but we wanted to discuss with you Kylie's situation, in person. So we can help her through this difficult time." The principal and counselor smiled at him sympathetically.

He wasn't even sure where to start. "Well, she's got no interest in basketball anymore. She doesn't want to hang out with her friends— or her friends aren't allowed to hang out with her, I'm not really sure. You know how pre-teens can be. And she's trying to process more than any twelve-year-old should be able to."

The counselor wrote as he spoke and the principal maintained eye contact with him, nodding slowly after each sentence.

"Does Kylie have any coping mechanisms? Any way to work through the trauma?"

Staring beyond them, he shook his head. "No, not really," he admitted. He started to feel self-conscious, like he hadn't been providing enough support for his daughter. "We spend time together," he added.

"Well, that's a great thing! But that isn't necessarily a coping mechanism. I'm talking about ways you can work through the grief. What about you? Do you have anything that helps you? We only ask because that could be a model for her."

He knew better than to say drinking. "Shelley used to journal daily. I do from time to time too. It helps me process my thoughts from the day."

The counselor, just landing on what she thought was a brilliant idea, seemed to perk up. "Well, what an excellent thing to share with Kylie! Maybe buy her a nice journal in her favorite color. It's a way to write out her feelings, and also have a connection with her mother."

Lyle agreed that this seemed to be an excellent idea.

When the meeting came to an end, the counselor excused herself and the principal asked Lyle to hang back for a moment. "Mr. Lazrin, I wanted to let you know that the detectives on your wife's case have been by the school several times."

He was genuinely surprised by this. "Several times? Why?"

Her shoulders went up in a slight shrug. "They say they are trying to learn more about her interactions...but it has been several times. Frankly, I'm finding it a bit disruptive at this point."

"Good God," he muttered.

"Yes. I'm not one to interfere with an investigation obviously but I think it's jarring for Kylie so I just..." and she leaned in lowering her voice. "I just wanted to make you were aware."

He thanked her and shook her hand before exiting the room.

Later that day, Kylie slid into the passenger's seat.

"I got you a gift." Lyle reached into the side door pocket and pulled out a small book that he handed to her. She examined the purple leather-bound journal with gold accents. He dug back in and pulled out a coordinating pen and handed that to her too.

She didn't say anything as the car line started to move. "I got it because—"

"I know why you got it," she said flatly.

He was worried she didn't like it. After they drove in silence for several minutes, he heard her sniffling.

"Thanks, Dad. I love it."

He took his eyes off the road for a brief second to smile at his daughter. He put his hand on her shoulder and gave it a squeeze before refocusing on the road. She cracked open the journal and was writing about her day. Kylie was so focused that she didn't notice that her father intentionally took the long way to avoid the defaced billboard.

Later that night, Lyle walked into his daughter's room, where she was again writing in her journal, Gus Gus laying beside her purring. *Maybe they would be okay after all*, he thought....

Chapter Thirty-Eight

June 2025

EACH DAY WAS INCREASINGLY MORE difficult without Shelley there. Lyle's guilt grew like a cancer. He was starting to withdraw into himself. He'd force himself to get up and take Kylie to and from school but that was basically it. He wasn't showering, he was barely eating, unless shots of vodka counted as a meal.

"Dad, can you please, I don't know, do something today?" his daughter complained as she stood above him.

"Hmm?" He looked up at his daughter. He had fallen asleep on the couch. It was 4pm on a Tuesday.

"I don't want to be rude, but maybe shower and get dressed? Go outside. Do something."

Lyle pushed himself up on the couch and she sat next to him.

"I know mom's not here but I still am." She looked over at her father to see his reaction.

He took in a deep breath and held it there. Inside, he shattered into a million pieces. Lyle wrapped his arm around his daughter and drew her into him. "I'm so sorry, kiddo. Let's get out of the house, spend some quality time together. Why don't we get some pizza?"

Kylie gave a weak smile. "Dad, we've had pizza nearly every night for weeks. I don't think I can eat another pizza...maybe ever again. But I wouldn't mind some pasta."

He tossed around her words, *I'm still here.* They kept repeating in his head. This was the wake-up call he needed. Even with this oppressive sadness and guilt pressing down on him, he had to be there for his daughter.

Soon they were in the car on the way to Asbury Park. Lyle was cleaned up and dressed. Showering and putting on clean clothes actually felt really good and he regretted spending so much time wallowing. He could feel just that small adjustment helped to lift his mood a bit. They walked through the door of the seafood restaurant and sat at a table in the corner.

There was something weighing on his mind that he wanted to ask her about. He was worried she'd take it the wrong way though. "Ky, do you think we should talk to someone?"

"Like a therapist?"

"Yeah, I think we have a lot to work out, and to work through," he responded, treading carefully.

Kylie thought for a moment and then nodded her head. "I think that might be a good idea."

He was pleasantly surprised by this and looked forward to working on scheduling the sessions. They needed to start the path toward healing.

The waitress handed them the large menus with little cartoon lobsters in the corner. Kylie quickly found what she wanted—shrimp scampi. Lyle hadn't made up his mind so quickly.

He continued to read over it when he noticed out of the corner of his eye—bright red hair. Lyle froze. He couldn't believe she had showed up here, with his daughter.

"Kylie, you know what. I think you were right, Italian food sounds much better." Kylie looked at him like she couldn't believe it.

"We are already here, Dad. Don't be weird. Anyway, they have pasta here!"

Lyle stood up tossing a few $20s on the table. "Let's go," he said urgently, ignoring her look of confusion.

Lyle apologized to the host and quickly ushered his daughter into the car.

"What the hell was that?" his daughter asked as she buckled her seatbelt.

"Watch your language, please. We are going for Italian food—like you asked for."

Kylie grimaced at her father and he set the address into the GPS.

"Philly! Why the he..."

He shot her a look and then quickly pulled out of the parking lot.

"Why are we going to Philly? There has to be five hundred Italian places between here and Philly."

Lyle was aware of his eccentric behavior but he couldn't calm himself down. What the hell was she doing there? Was she following them? Would she be crazy enough to follow them all the way to Philly? Or maybe he was the crazy one and he was over-reacting? She was allowed to eat seafood in the next town over. It wasn't a crime. Lyle's mind ping ponged between anxiety and doubt.

Regardless of the situation, he had the overwhelming urge to get the hell out of town. He sped up, going ten to fifteen miles over the speed limit. "We are going to Philly because I know of a really amazing Italian place that I always wanted to try. And tonight seems like a great night for it."

She sighed loudly to express she was annoyed but didn't fully object.

Over an hour later they found a parking garage and walked to the restaurant, Kylie making her displeasure known the whole way. Once inside, Lyle looked around, scanning for that familiar face. The host greeted them. "Can we have a table in the back? Actually, no near the door." Lyle didn't look but knew his daughter would be looking at him quizzically.

"Sure!" Beamed the host, unaware of his heightened anxiety.

After sliding into the red leather booths, the waitress handed them the menus. They peered over each section with endless delicious choices and both of their stomachs started to growl. It was nearly fifteen minutes of scanning the restaurant before he was able to settle in a bit. Kylie ordered spaghetti and meatballs, a dish probably not worth driving this far for, Lyle thought. He ordered vodka rigatoni, white wine, and garlic bread to share.

"I want to revisit the idea of going away for a weekend."

Kylie swirled her fork in the pasta, watching it go around and around. "Isn't this a getaway? You drove me an hour for some pasta."

"Don't get smart, Kylie. What do you think? It would be good for both of us to—I don't know—reset."

"Yeah, let's do it. I feel like I need to get away from—everything."

They chatted smoothly for the next hour about school and the trip. All the while, Lyle was still keeping his eye on the door, his leg bobbing up and down a mile a minute.

Kylie was noticing his skittish behavior but decided not to comment. Sometimes he'd freeze momentarily. His eyes scanned the restaurant continuously. When the dessert came, two plates of tiramisu, she thought, *he thinks the cops are coming for him*. And though she tried to pretend she hadn't thought it, ashamed of herself, for a fraction of a second, she too thought it was possible.

Excerpt from the personal diary of Kylie Lazrin

I think I'm going crazy. I'm going back and forth between thinking there is zero percent chance he did it, to being very, very unsure.

He did it:

- Eye twitching

- Closes laptop when I come by

- Dating?

- Everyone thinks he did it

He didn't do it:

- Loved mom

- Wouldn't take mom from me ... right?

- Never hurt a fly

.... I just don't know.

Chapter Thirty-Nine

LYLE HAD BECOME INCREASINGLY frustrated that the cops were no help. He decided to make contact with a local private investigator that he found online.

Sitting across a wooden desk was a balding man. The room smelled of smoke masked by air freshener and it stung his lungs. In his office they went over all the details from the beginning.

"So, do you think you can help me?"

"Yeah, absolutely. I'll have my partner keep an eye on your house, see if we can catch whatever is happening there. I'll be in charge of looking into what happened to your wife."

They shook hands and Lyle felt a small glimmer of hope. He was grasping at anything at this point.

The summer tourists were slowly starting to trickle in as the air had started to warm. Residents were out in droves after the long winter. Lyle parked his car, passing the PI sitting across the street. His phone buzzed.

"Yeah?"

"Mr. Lazrin, it's been a week. There hasn't been any activity at your house. I'm just checking in to see if you want the surveillance still."

He thought for a moment as money was extremely tight at this point. Then he thought of his daughter, alone with the door unlocked. He asked for it to continue, knowing he'd have to start relying on credit cards to get by soon and then typed into his to-do list 'cancel trip'.

He had known for a long time that the trip wouldn't happen, and despite needing the money, it was a difficult decision. Shelley had worked so long on that trip—his throat constricted at the thought of wiping that all away.

"I spoke with the two detectives on your case. They weren't too happy that you hired a PI."

Lyle chuckled. "Yeah, I could see that pissing off Detective Derzo. Were they willing to collaborate at all?"

"I get the feeling they won't want to play ball. But we will see..."

Lyle said goodbye to the PI and sent over the funds for an additional week of surveillance, as he watched his bank account dwindle to an alarming number. Then he sank into his couch. Whoever had been breaking in must know that the PI is there and that's why they had stopped coming into his home, taking his things and robbing him of feeling secure in his own place.

Chapter Forty

LYLE SAT in the office waiting for the detectives.

Derzo entered and sat down, reaching for the recording device. He hit record and started asking a series of questions.

Lyle's thoughts seemed to be split in two directions, he was answering the officer's questions but continuously trying to run through everything that had happened so far. His mind thought back to the notifications from Shelley's phone and how, if they had just been able to track it, they could have a clue that might lead them to whoever took her.

"And what happened after that?" Derzo asked.

"How many times do I need to go over the same thing? Listen, I don't know why you can't get help from a bigger agency or at least work with the PI I hired."

Derzo looked at him skeptically. "Why would we need that?"

"Because it seems you can't get basic shit done here!"

Derzo's face flashed red with anger. "We are working very hard to find out what happened to your wife, Mr. Lazrin."

"Well, if you worked with a bigger agency, maybe you'd have the technology to track where Shelley's notifications were coming from?"

"Lyle, what the hell are you talking about?"

"I told Petrov that Shelley's location had been shared twice. I asked her to track it and she said it wasn't possible."

Derzo let out a long and loud breath. "Jesus Christ," he muttered.

"Go ahead and ask her. Where's Detective Petrov?"

The officer paused the recording device and leaned back in his chair. He coughed and shifted a bit in his seat. "She's no longer on this case. For now, you'll just be meeting with me."

Lyle's eyes narrowed. "Why?"

"Come on, Lyle. You know I can't get into information like that with you."

"Well, if it has something to do with my case I sure deserve to know."

"I'm not at liberty to say."

Lyle sat back in the seat shaking his head. Whatever was happening at this station, he didn't trust anyone—not to help his wife, not to find the truth and not to pin this on him.

"Fine, let me ask this another way. Was there any mishandling of my case by anyone involved?"

Derzo chuckled. "That's an even worse way to ask it."

Lyle looked at him with a death stare. "Listen—I thought I was going crazy but maybe I wasn't. Sometimes, I felt like she was, I don't know how to say it—flirting with me?"

Derzo let out a large exhale. "All I will say is, sometimes we get a little too set on one scenario and then we try very hard to make everything else fit. And...perhaps that is why she is on another case."

Lyle went to open his mouth to ask another question.

"And that is all I will say!" Derzo repeated more sternly.

Lyle started to piece together some things that had happened. He wasn't sure if he was completely off base but had to ask. "You can track her phone here, can't you?"

"Of course we can, Lyle."

Lyle didn't know what, or who, to believe anymore.

Chapter Forty-One

THIS WOULD HAVE BEEN the time of year that Shelley would have gotten their beach passes for the season. Another reminder of all the little things she did that kept everything running smoothly. Lyle decided to lace up his sneakers and go buy the passes.

"Can I help you?" Asked the woman behind the counter.

"I'll take three season passes, please."

The woman told him the amount, and he filled out the check, knowing he had barely enough to cover it. He just couldn't bring himself to only order two. As he walked away from the booth, he got a call from the PI.

"Hello?"

"Yeah, Lyle, I've been at your house and there is a suspicious woman who has been walking near your property. Might be nothing, I'll keep an eye on it but I'm going to send over a few photos."

He hung up and sat on a bench. Immediately, his eyes were drawn to her hair.

Lyle got home completely drained. He had zero energy and just gazed at the wall until everything became a little blurry. There was a nagging feeling, like something wasn't right. It was pecking at him but he couldn't figure out what it was. He replayed all the events. And then it hit him.

The strange behavior.

The vanilla perfume.

Being removed from the case.

Wandering near his home.

He flipped through the unsolicited texts he got and zoomed in to each one. There it was, just a sliver, her unmistakable fiery hair.

He opened his laptop and logged into his wife's Facebook profile. He typed in the name Trina Petrov. He scoured through the different profiles, trying to isolate them to searches for New Jersey. That was a dead end.

Then he recalled his wife had been talking to someone before she disappeared. He opened up the messages and searched. He read through their messages again. The woman had mentioned that her child was on the middle school swim team—there was no swim team until high school. Could this be a catfish account?

The day before she disappeared, the woman had tried to get Shelley to meet up for coffee, when she declined, she asked if they could meet for lunch. Shelley hadn't responded.

His hands shook while he typed as if they were the ground during an earthquake. His gut told him, whoever was behind this account was an imposter. They had been using the facade of motherhood to lure Shelley...and he knew who he thought the catfish was. The woman's profile was created a few months back. All the pictures hid her face and she wore what was obviously a wig. "God damn," he muttered.

Lyle decided to make contact.

Hey Kitty Kat. It's me, he typed, his hand hovering over the send button. Lyle swallowed what felt like a rock in his throat before closing his eyes and pushing send. He stared at the screen for several minutes waiting for her to respond. If he was wrong, he was going to seriously fuck up everything.

An eternity passed as he waited for a signal that they were typing back—but nothing. And then it happened—a call from an unknown number came in. The sound made him jump because he was so on edge.

Lyle could barely grip his phone as his hands trembled. He hovered over the accept button for several seconds before pushing it. His chest was rising and falling at a dizzying rate. He felt unwell but managed a, "Hello?" and waited for a response.

On the other end he heard her loudly breathing and then finally, "I was waiting for you," she cooed.

He instantly recognized her voice.

"Why did you leave the restaurant? I wanted to be with you."

"Come on, you know you can't do that. I had my daughter with me. You know we can't be together like that, not yet." Lyle felt the undulation of his lunch creeping up and down his esophagus. He shoved it down and made himself go to another place mentally.

"I know, but I really, really, wanted to be with you," she said, her words smooth and sweet like honey.

"You will. Very soon. I need to know. The thing with Shelley, was that you?"

"I didn't do anything," she said but then a soft giggle left her lips.

"Come on Kitty Kat...tell me what you did for me. It gets me going, thinking of you—that you did something like that for me."

"I'm glad you called, Lyle. I'm glad we can be together now."

"Me too, Kat. Me too." He hung up the phone and ran to the bathroom, throwing himself over the sink, where he released everything he had been holding in. The anticipation of it all was too much to handle.

I meet with Ms. Katrina Petrov for a six hour session. During our time together, she insisted the entire time that she was in a serious relationship with Lyle. She recounted how she met Lyle at the grocery store and he commented on her headband. She recognized him from a local billboard around town as he is a prominent real estate agent.

He also commented to Ms. Petrov about how difficult his wife is. It was at that moment that Ms. Petrov felt they entered into a relationship. She left her groceries and followed him home. She felt that his commentary about his wife, painting her in a negative light, was a call for her to help him get rid of his wife so they could be together.

Using Mr. Lazrin's profession to her advantage, she was able to gain access to his work phone number. She portrayed herself as a possible client at one point and arranged a meeting. She became nervous and left before making contact.

As Ms. Petrov was also a detective in Belmar and exhibited a high level of intelligence, she was very knowledgeable about crime scenes. She does not admit to using this knowledge in a nefarious manner.

She was also able to have regular contact with Lyle as part of the investigation, which she further fantasized as being part of their relationship.

She was able to gain entry into his home on several occasions. Being familiar with his camera set up, she was able to avoid detection. Despite going through the effort to remain undetected, she still sees it as being invited in. However, there is no discussion of Lyle inviting her. Ms. Petrov said she snuck into the home and stole a photo album that belonged to Lyle's daughter. She then took all family photos and replaced Shelley's face with her own.

It was of great concern that Ms. Petrov also viewed Mr. and Mrs. Lazrin's daughter as her own. She entered the middle school and left her mother's necklace. It was a locket and she had replaced the photo with a note. She then made contact with the child and offered to give her a ride home.

In Ms. Petrov's mind, this was further evidence of her connection to the family, and she viewed this as a mother taking her child home from school. Despite the fact that, once the ride was over, she had no further contact with the child, she was still processing this event as her morphing into the child's mother.

At some point, Lyle was in the station and mentioned that without a body, the investigation couldn't continue properly. Ms. Petrov saw this as a plea from Lyle to kill his wife so he could move on with his life. Ms. Petrov was adamant that this would be the catalyst to their life together.

When prompted further about it, she still continued to deny involvement in Ms. Lazrin's disappearance.

However, she became more bold in her actions—such as following Lyle and his daughter when they were out. Ms. Petrov complained that at some point Lyle hired a private investigator so she could not come and go as she pleased in his home and neighborhood.

Despite telling me all this, Ms. Petrov denies killing Shelley Lazrin but emphasized that she would have. I believe this is further proof of her delusions.

From our discussion, I do not believe that Lyle had any interactions with Ms. Petrov that would have led her on. All of these situations were momentary interactions that she created an elaborate narrative for which never happened.

It is my conclusion that Ms. Petrov suffers from an extreme case of De Clerambault's syndrome, more commonly known as erotomania. With this condition, a person believes they are in a romantic relationship with a person they may have never met, had little contact with, or a celebrity. They experience strong delusions that the feelings they are having are reciprocated.

In conclusion, it is my professional opinion to recommend that

Ms. Petrov should receive lifelong treatment for this condition as well as medication. What happened to Shelley Lazrin will have to be left to the police, as she made no formal confession to me. Mr. Lazrin and his daughter should be made aware of her whereabouts at all times so he can take proper safety precautions.

I met with Lyle Lazrin today for our third session. He is understandably experiencing intense grief at the passing of his wife, Shelley. He had been experiencing rage in a previous session, which seemed to subside during this session. I asked him if he harbored any animosity towards his wife's killer and he responded, "Not anymore." I asked Lyle, "What caused that change?" He refused to answer. I found this very curious but as he would not elaborate, it is something I will have to try to explore with him at a later time when he is ready.

During our previous session, it seemed as if he was experiencing intense paranoia. Lyle had commented often that he felt like he was being watched and that things were going missing from his home. He seemed far more relaxed this session and did not mention any of the previously stated situations.

At this time, I do not know the cause of that change.

Overall, I feel that during this session he has shown remarkable improvement.

Chapter Forty-Two

THE TIME WAS FINALLY right for their getaway to the Poconos. Lyle thought he had timed it perfectly.

Lyle and Kylie tossed their bags onto the wooden floor and explored the small cabin. Kylie had brought a stack of books and her journal. Lyle had brought a fishing magazine and some board games. This short trip was going to be all about relaxing and getting away from it all.

Kylie, a notorious over-packer, looked at the stack of fantasy books she brought and hoped they would take her to somewhere far off and magical. Some place where it hurt less.

The owners of the cabin kindly allowed them to bring their 'emotional support' cat and Gus Gus made himself right at home. He hopped onto the hunter green couch and fell asleep in a little ball immediately.

The cabin had a room with a large queen bed and another with bunk beds. Lyle watched his daughter as she unpacked the small bag. A stuffed pink rabbit was the first thing to come out.

He smiled, though it was filled with sadness. Shelley had given her that rabbit on her first birthday. It was both touching and heartbreaking that she couldn't be away from it for even two nights—

especially considering she had only taken it out of the closet once Shelley left.

"Dad, can I stay with you tonight?" The rabbit held close to her chest, she seemed so little right now.

"Sweetie, you are getting a bit too old for that. How about I stay the first night in the bunk bed just until you fall asleep? Once you go to sleep, I'll go to my room, because that bed is going to destroy my back."

Reluctantly, she agreed to the compromise.

The two settled in quickly and Lyle asked her to help him make their dinner. "We are going to make pesto and pasta tonight, sounds good?"

"Sure, I'll help," she said, reaching for the fresh basil and washing it in the sink. Lyle began to dice garlic and he looked over at his daughter.

"Is school getting any better?"

She continued to pluck the little leaves off the stem one by one before responding. "I mean...maybe. Once the funeral was announced kids stopped saying things to my face. But I think they are still talking about it. Now they probably do it behind my back." She looked pained as she explained the situation.

He knew middle school was difficult for anyone but couldn't even imagine what she must be going through. He shook his head in disgust. "Kids can be really cruel. I'm sorry."

"Dad, I understand you want to check in on me right now. I get it. But can we not talk about this for the weekend. Can we just pretend to be okay?"

Lyle nodded his head, tossing the basil she picked and the garlic into the food processor. "Okay," he agreed. He added the remaining ingredients and watched them as they all melded together.

They sat at the small wooden table eating their dinner quietly. Their silence allowed them to hear the scurrying of squirrels in the trees outside their cabin. Kylie pushed her food around on the plate, occasionally taking small, slow bites. Lyle desperately wanted to know how she was coping but he had agreed not to ask. The questions he wanted answers to kept gnawing at him and he couldn't think of anything else to say.

"This came out good."

"Yeah," she said flatly, not looking up from her plate.

"Thanks for your help."

"Yup."

He gave up. Together they cleaned up and Lyle put on his favorite playlist. Bruce Springsteen's voice and guitar filled the air. Lyle sang along as he cleaned the utensils.

"Ugh, Dad. This is old people music."

Lyle dropped the utensils in the sink and dramatically pretended to be offended. "You know, I think it's illegal to make comments like that in New Jersey."

"Well then, I guess it's good for me that we are currently in PA."

"Well surely they won't let you back in with comments like that."

They grinned at each other.

The track switched to Jersey Girl and he held out his hand. At first, she rolled her eyes but then she took it. He twirled her around, like he had when she was little. She laughed and it was a moment of pure joy. For a split second, everything was okay.

"I don't want her to just be a memory." Lyle pulled his daughter towards him and kissed the top of her head.

"I'm scared."

"You don't have anything to be scared of. They will find who did this very soon. They will never be able to hurt us or anyone else ever again. I promise."

"No, it's not that, though. I'm scared of all the big moments. I'm scared of how everything I was supposed to look forward to will have this big gaping void without her, when she should have been there to help me plan it, celebrate in it. You know my bat mitzvah is next year. How will you help me with that?"

"We will figure it out. Your mother is always with you, Kylie. In your determination. In your love for trying new things. Every moment you spent together formed you to be the girl you are today and the woman you will become. She will never leave you." He hugged her tight and he felt her relax a little.

"And I'm sure your grandparents will be more than happy to help you with the aspects of the bat mitzvah that I don't understand. I'll learn what I need to so I can help out as much as possible too. But we will make the best of it and find a way to honor your mother."

"Thanks, dad. I like that idea." She got on her tippy toes and gave him a kiss on the cheek, something she hadn't done since she was little.

They grew silent and all that could be heard was the music. The iconic raspy voice sang: *She let you into the parts of herself that'll bring you down.* Lyle bolted to the speaker and turned off the music. "Maybe you're right, no more music," he said as he turned to smile at her.

"She loved you, Dad. You know that, right?"

He turned away from her, hiding the tears that threatened to trickle down his face. Lyle nodded and the tears that rimmed his eyes flowed. He swatted them away like a fly.

He got up, trying to hide from the vulnerability of the moment. Lyle lit a flame in the fireplace. They both sat reading as the wood crackled. Gus Gus loudly purred by Kylie's side. The light sound of rain started pattering on the roof and it added to the cozy feeling. The pair read for several hours while drinking hot chocolate. It should have been a moment of deep comfort but an underlying sadness filled each second.

Darkness began to envelope the sky. Kylie yawned loudly.

"Time for bed?" Lyle asked.

"Yeah, probably. My eyes are getting so heavy that it's hard to keep reading."

She went off to bed and Lyle sat on the wooden floor waiting for her to fall asleep as promised. As she tossed in the bed, hugging the rabbit, he turned down the light on his phone. He flipped open the unread text messages he had gotten recently.

There were thirty-two photos. Lyle's heart was pounding as he flipped through them.

The first one was innocent enough. He swiped to the next one and it shocked him. Bright red hair, twirling down a thin, petite frame, her skin the color of porcelain. He quickly closed his phone, feeling extremely awkward having seen that image while in the same room as his daughter.

When her tossing stopped, he went into his own room and reopened the photos. Each one was more suggestive than the next. His body flashed with heat and he smiled mischievously. He had a plan.

Many hours later, the light rain had turned into a deluge. The water droplets pounded the roof and it woke Kylie up. She bolted up in bed when there was a large crack of thunder. She slowly walked through the darkened room searching for the light switch.

Kylie left the room and went to knock on her dad's door. "Dad? Can I stay with you? I'm, kinda, scared." He didn't respond, so she knocked louder. The only response was another crack of thunder and her anxiety skyrocketed. "Dad!" And she pounded her fist on the door until it hurt. She then slowly opened the door and called for him again. She flicked on the light switch and approached his bed slowly. His bed was empty.

With no parent there to reprimand her, she exclaimed, "What the fuck!"

She walked over to the windows that looked out onto the porch. The wind howled and she doubted he'd be outside. She moved the curtain back the smallest bit to look for him but again was met with emptiness. She could see his car was still in the muddy driveway. "Where the fuck did he go?" she said to Gus Gus who laid at the foot of the bed.

She went back into the main room, checked that the door was

locked, and threw a chair in front of the door to the cabin. Then Kylie ran to her room and crawled under the covers.

A wave of grief washed over her. Her father's absence triggered the memory of the days when her mother first vanished, those first moments of uncertainty. Kylie went into a full panic attack when she thought she might never see her father again. She lay there shaking with fear, her chest heaving up and down. "I'll wait until sunrise and then I'll go find help," she told herself.

However, she didn't have to wait that long. The sound of the cabin door creaking open very, very, slowly could be heard, the chair being dragged with it. Kylie sucked in her breath and cursed herself for not coming up with a better security plan.

Unsure of who had entered the home, she didn't want to make a sound, not even breathing. Footsteps light and intentional could be heard, but they weren't going towards her room. They were going to her fathers. She sat in bed all night, not moving, barely breathing, waiting for morning.

Excerpt from the personal diary entry of Kylie Lazrin, Friday June 13, 2025

What the actual fuck just happened?

Chapter Forty-Three

Three hours earlier...

KATRINA PETROV LAID IN BED, snuggled beneath her warm covers as the rain fell heavily outside. She had taken a sleeping pill earlier in the day and was just having the effects wear off. She'd pop another one soon. Her life was falling apart, she'd lost her job and after all she had done, she was still alone. Sleeping the night and day away helped ease her growing frustration.

A light noise made her stir in bed. A sliver of light cracked through her bedroom door, followed by light footsteps. "Who... who's there?" she asked, alarmed. She tried to squirm to the other side of the bed where the nightstand held a small pocket-knife.

"Come on...you know, Kitty Kat," said a familiar voice, somehow both sweet and villainous at the same time.

Katrina had been clenching her cover but the sound of his voice let her relax her grip. The minimal amount of light from the hallway was just enough to make out part of his face. This couldn't be happening she thought. "Lyle?" she asked hopefully into the darkness.

There was no response, but the footsteps grew closer and she felt both terrified and excited. When he was next to her bed, she could feel him staring at her, though she could no longer see his features. She cleared her throat. "You finally came."

He laughed. "Finally? This was the first chance I got."

She could hear him move away from the opposite side of the bed. He came around and was now right beside her. He was so close, his breathing was audible. Katrina took in a deep inhale, savoring his familiar woodsy scent that had been captivating her for months.

When he was right above her, he peeled back the cover. She lay there in overly baggy sweatpants—definitely not what she would have picked for this moment. The red lace undergarments that she had photographed herself in to entice him lay just a few feet away. "Can I change?" she asked in her soft voice. He didn't acknowledge her.

She felt Lyle's hand roaming her body over her thick clothing. It sent hot shivers through her that awakened parts of her she hadn't felt before. The space between her legs pulsated and grew warmer as he moved his hand around, exploring her. She thought she'd explode when he moved them underneath her sweatshirt. Katrina lifted her hips instinctively, yearning for what she knew would come next.

"Is this what you wanted?" he said, almost purring.

His voice was deep and sexy. Katrina had lost her ability to speak, she just nodded but he couldn't see her.

"I said, is this what you want?" His voice was forceful now.

"Yes!" she nearly screamed.

"Sit up, I'm going to make you beg for it."

She obeyed, willing to do whatever he wanted. Katrina's mind and body were completely at his will.

"Get up, and sit over there," he said pointing to the small desk in the corner.

Momentarily she was confused.

"Go!" he barked.

Again, she followed his orders without a thought or question.

There was a small lamp on the desk and he turned it on, casting a small amount of light in the corner of the room, like a single lamp in a dark alley way. He noticed a fuzzy cat headband laying on the small table. Where had he seen those?

Her bright red curls cascaded over her shoulders. He ran his hands through her hair—it was truly beautiful. Lyle continued to use his hands to explore her body—from her hair to her shoulder and then slowly slid down.

Katrina closed her eyes, blocking out everything else around her so she could just take in the sensation of his warm, strong hands. She sucked in a breath when he reached her chest. Though she was in her early thirties, she had never been touched there before.

She reached for him. Her hand landed on his thigh and moved up his leg until she landed at her desired destination. He closed his eyes and tilted back his head. Lyle hadn't been touched in months and a small moan escaped. It was several moments before he moved her hand away.

He tugged at the neckline of her sweatshirt, exposing a small tattoo—a heart with an L in it. It was all the confirmation he needed.

"Pick up the pen and write what I say," he demanded and she nodded.

"I killed Shelley Lazrin. I'm sorry for the pain I have caused her friends and family."

"No, I'm not writing that," she said, shaking her head.

"Do it," he bellowed.

"Lyle, not until you tell me why?"

"Why what?"

"Why do you want me to write that? You're scaring me."

"Don't be scared," he said as he leaned into her, inhaling her scent. Vanilla.

He left her there with a pen in hand. She watched his every move, like predator and prey.

Her eyes followed him as he walked over to the closet and opened the door. Perched on the edge of the seat, she braced herself for his reaction.

As soon as he flicked on the light, he murmured, "Oh, my god." There, hanging in the closet was all of Shelley's clothing, methodically organized in the exact way it had been in their home. Lyle shook his head, running his hands along the fabric.

He turned back to her still sitting at the desk. "And the photo album? Do you have that too?"

She nodded nervously as he began to approach her, each footstep heavy and intimidating.

She stood up, hoping to embrace him, to have him touch her again. A desperation pulled at her; She had never needed anything more badly in her life. Her desire for him was animalistic at this point. His look back at her was hollow and she wanted to turn back time to just a few seconds ago, when he was learning every part of her body.

"I need you to admit what you did, to prove to me how much I mean to you. That you'd literally do anything for me."

"You know I would," she said on the verge of tears.

He leaned in so his lips were just touching hers. As he spoke, she could feel the warmth from his breath. "Then do what I asked you to do."

She picked up the pen, trembling. A moment of hesitation and then Katrina wrote as she was directed to do. She was so close to getting what she had been trying to achieve for months, nothing would stand in her way now.

Once she was done, she looked up at him. "I'm ready. For you."

"Shut up and get in the bed."

The moment she was waiting for was here and she almost couldn't contain how excited it made her. A shiver ran down her spine and her whole body lit on fire. "Lyle, I want you to take me right here and now," she said looking him straight in the eye.

"That's exactly what I came here to do. Now lay the fuck down, Katrina."

"Call me Kat," she whispered.

"I'll call you what I want. Now LAY down," he commanded.

Katrina laid down. Between her thighs tightened with anticipation. "I've never done this before. Is this going to hurt?"

"Absolutely."

She watched him staring at her with cold eyes, unmoving.

"Take me, now," she said, begging.

He continued to glare at her.

"What? What is it, Lyle?"

No response.

"Are you okay? Are you upset with me?"

Nothing.

"Stop, you are scaring me. Why won't you talk to me?... Is this about the baby?"

"The...." His voice trailed off in confusion.

Katrina was thrilled that he finally uttered a word to her, so she began speaking quickly, accelerating like a car onto the highway.

"I took her so we could be together. It's what you wanted."

Lyle's face became stone.

"I did it for you, Lyle. I took her, but I didn't know she was pregnant! I swear. She didn't know either. I kept her here for weeks and, well, it became clear. But I couldn't let her go. Not when we needed to be together. And you asked me to end it all so you could move on. I was only doing what you asked." She waited as he stood strong and solid, like a statue.

"It's okay! Please, don't be angry…We can have another one! Together," she offered, as she noticed Lyle's eyes widened so large, it was all she could see.

"Or we don't have to! I'll do anything to be with you, please just say something to me," she begged, tears running down her face. "It was all for you."

Lyle ran his hands over his forehead with increasing intensity.

"Stop, you're going to hurt yourself. Come, lay down with me."

There were several orange pill bottles on her counter. He read each one and then he leaned over and dumped them into his hand. She felt Lyle's fingers enter her mouth. He forcefully jammed something down her throat and she gagged. Undeterred, he did it several more times.

"Lyle, please. Give me what you came for." She managed to whisper as she reached for him but he stepped back.

Katrina's vision began to blur a bit. "How many did you give me?"

He could see her trembling—and it surprised him that he liked it. He wasn't sure if it was desire, fear or both, but it excited him. Lyle moved to a chair in the corner, tears streaking his face and watched as she slowly drifted in and out of consciousness. The sound of his sniffling was the only thing that could be heard, as she went still.

Lyle left the room and walked back in now wearing blue gloves, gripping a small but sharp kitchen knife. He sat back in the chair and twirled it in his hand as he watched her fight to keep her eyes open. Before her confession, he wasn't positive he would actually be able to do it. Now he was eager for what was next.

She watched him, barely awake, like it was in slow motion, as Lyle leaned down and whispered in her ear. "You took everything from me. Things I didn't even know I had. I'm going to do the same."

He had an overwhelming desire to spit on her like the piece of trash she was, but he knew he couldn't leave any evidence. By all accounts, he was over two hours away right now in the Poconos with his daughter. If he hoped to get away with his plan, he couldn't leave any evidence to contradict that.

Katrina heard the sound of him walking towards the bed again but at this point was too weak to move. She watched as Lyle picked up her limp wrist and slid the knife into her hand. He cupped his gloved hand around hers and then dug it into the skin on her other wrist and dragged it across. The straight, clean line flashed red and then began to flow over.

There was no pain, only confusion and disappointment. It felt like she was hanging above herself, watching as the man she loved drained her of life. She was so sick that she couldn't even be upset. She loved him deeply, obsessively, and nothing would change that.

The last thing she said to him as he watched her dying was, "Thank you, Love." And as she weaved in and out of consciousness, she thought of Lyle and how they would be together someday on the other side.

Lyle asked me why I listen to true crime so much. "Doesn't it bother you? All the blood and tragedy?" he asked me. Yeah, me and the millions of other women obsessed with true crime! I asked him if he was worried I was getting ideas. He sorta laughed but said we'd be together forever. I said, "Until death does she part." He didn't find that funny. He got real serious with me. Told me he loved me and that he and Kylie needed me. "If you are having thoughts like that, you need to talk to someone," he implored me. I know he's worried about my mental health, so I decided to give therapy a try again. Hopefully it goes better than last time.

But when do I have time to see someone? I'm not sure if it's the anxiety or I'm getting sick but I have been so, so tired lately. Whenever no one is in the house, I go straight to bed. Just another thing I have to deal with...

Chapter Forty-Four

AS THE SUN began to extend its reach into her cabin room, Kylie stayed exactly where she had been for the past few hours, frozen with fear. She could hear footsteps again in her father's room and then there was a knock on her door. It made her heart stop.

She didn't answer.

"Kylie? You awake?" It was the familiar voice of her father and a wave of relief spread over her.

She quickly bolted for the door and gave him a big hug.

"Hey, kiddo! You okay?"

She just squeezed him harder. "There was a big storm last night and it was scary. Kept me up all night."

"Aw, I'm sorry. You should have woken me up. I would have stayed up with you."

Her relief was replaced by suspicion. Kylie's eyebrows rose in question but her head was still buried in his shoulder. "Yeah, you're right. I will next time."

He kissed the top of her head. "Come on. I'll make a full breakfast —bacon, pancakes—"

"With chocolate chips?" She kept telling herself to keep cool, act normal.

"You got it!"

She watched as he walked into the kitchen area. Kylie wasn't taking her eyes off him for the rest of the trip. As he cooked, the smell of coffee, bacon and pancakes filled the air but nothing could calm her jitters. Where had her father been last night? And why did he lie about it?

Over breakfast she asked her father, "Did you sleep okay last night?" She prayed her voice didn't betray her.

"I did. That bed is pretty comfy. I love the sound of rain, helps put me right to sleep. How about you? Were you okay before the thunder started?" He took a big swig of his coffee, finishing the cup. He immediately got up and refilled it.

Kylie was confused as to why her dad would lie to her. It made her nervous but she decided not to confront him about it. "Yeah, I slept like a log until the storm!" And she forced a smile at her father. He grinned back, but there was something distant in his eyes. He reached for the salt and she noticed the bottle tremble in his hands.

What the hell are you keeping from me? she thought to herself.

Suddenly, she wasn't hungry anymore. She pushed around the food as her father ate.

Lyle thought about how Katrina would be found soon, and while he was able to convince his daughter that he had been in the cabin, soon he'd have to avoid the cops, the media, the public. The thought of it, and the overwhelming amount of coffee he had pumping through his body to fight off the fatigue, made him jittery.

"Dad!"

Lyle looked up and she pointed to his eye which was rapidly twitching. He had hoped she wouldn't have noticed. Instinctively, he raised his hand to cover it. "Sorry it's just a tick."

"A nervous tick. Are you okay?"

"It's not a nervous tick, it's just, emotions are running high still. It happens a lot lately."

Bullshit, she thought. She hated that she felt suspicious of her dad, but something was very wrong right now and she needed some separation to process it all.

"Can I go to grandma and grandpa's for a few days after this?" She was hatching a plan and knew until she had answers that she didn't want to stay with her dad.

"I'm already letting you take off Monday to be here...but I guess I could let you miss another day or two. I think the school will understand. Anyway, it's almost summer break—you're probably just watching movies." Lyle welcomed the idea of having a day or two kid free, in case he needed to cover his tracks...or if they came to arrest him.

Hello again journal.

Another day, same worries.

My dad bought me this diary and some glittery gel pens to go with it. It's so pretty. He hopes I'll write about my feelings but I don't think he wants to know what I'm feeling. I've had people telling me he is guilty for months and I have defended him at every turn. But after a while, when you hear things over and over, that can change the way you see things.

Did my dad love my mom? Yeah, I think so. Did they have the perfect marriage? Hell no. But show me anyone who does?

And as much as I want to think there is a zero percent chance, I can't push down this nagging feeling. Because there are things I just don't get... like why does he shut down his laptop whenever I walk in and he is on Facebook? It's super suspicious. I swear to God, if he is dating already I'll never speak to him again!

He doesn't think I notice but he's been drinking a lot more too. I found two vodka bottles in the recycling. Is he drinking more because he has a guilty conscience?

And worst of all- where did he go that night? Why did he lie about leaving the cabin? I still have another night here with him and to be honest, I'm a little nervous.

The police don't know who hurt my mom but they've always assumed it was my dad. I'm going to try to find out... no matter the consequences.

Chapter Forty-Five

KYLIE HAD BEGGED her dad to let her stay longer and longer at her grandparents. Finally, after a week she felt ready and asked them to drop her off at home. She got there early, knowing she had the house to herself. Her father was out showing houses again and she didn't expect him back for a few hours. Too many strange things had happened and she needed to know if her father had anything to do with it. For a while, everyone thought her dad did it, while part of her didn't think it was possible, everyone else's conviction had been starting to sway her.

She rummaged around in her dad's room trying to find anything. Under his bed she saw a small metal safe. Kylie first tried her birthday, then her mom's. No luck. She tried their anniversary and gained access. Inside was just a notebook. She flipped page after page, reading entries about the good days but also many about how much her father resented her mother. Each paragraph, each entry made her see her father in the same light that everyone else did. Her stomach clenched.

"My god," *he must have killed her*, she thought to herself.

Despite this thought, she continued reading, knowing she had to have every insight she possibly could to understand her father and her parents' relationship better. She got to the final entry, filled with disdain for her father.

"I wasn't sure I could do it- but I have no regrets. It looked like a suicide. There is no other way they can look at it. She had to suffer for what she did to Shelley and our family. My daughter was a light- that's been turned off. She could glow but chooses not to, too consumed by grief.

I got a call today from Derzo that I was no longer a suspect in Shelley's disappearance. Glad I'll never have to talk to that asshole again, or sit across from that psycho bitch.

They called me for an interview last night, and an article will come out tomorrow declaring it a suspected suicide.

I have no idea how life will go on from here, the guilt I will carry for what could have been. I pray daily for healing for Kylie. I've even started going to church- God knows I need redemption now. Hopefully our lives will go back to the monotony that my wife hated so much."

Kylie closed her dad's notebook and shook her head. "Son of a bitch," she said aloud to no one. Kylie thought back to the last weekend when they went away to the Poconos. It must have been the same weekend the detective had taken her life. Kylie remembered waking up from a nightmare and going to her father's room, but it was empty. She had gone back to her room, assuming her father's stress was bringing on insomnia and he was going for a long walk in the woods. But that had never fully made sense to her, either. When she heard the door click back at 3:30am, she never said anything to anyone.

Now it all made sense.

She left the room and rummaged around in her mother's craft supplies until she found an exacto knife. She carefully removed the final incriminating pages and tucked it under her arm. Kylie brought it into the living room, where family pictures hung everywhere, a happy life stolen from them because of one deranged woman's fantasy world. The anger she had been harboring towards her father transferred to the dead woman.

She was glad she was dead.

Kylie flicked the switch on the fireplace, wrapping the soft pink blanket her mother knitted around her. It was almost like a warm hug from her, as her hands had worked tirelessly for days to make this, each stitch filled with love. She watched the golden amber flames whip around then tossed the pages into the fire. She'd already lost one parent, she sure as hell wasn't going to lose the other. The flames quickly consumed the paper and she watched them burn, along with the only piece of evidence that existed of her father's misdeeds.

Her whole body relaxed and she felt a sense of peace all around her.

She went back and placed the journal in the safe and locked it. A weight lifted off her shoulders. She shoved the safe back under the bed and waited for her dad to return home.

A former local police officer, Katrina Petrov, known as Trina, was found dead this morning around 8am in her home. She had been let go from the police department days earlier for the mishandling of evidence.

The police responded to a call from her neighbor. They called to say she hadn't seen Ms. Petrov in a couple of days.

"She's usually sitting on her porch all day, flipping through some photo album. Didn't matter the weather, she was out there. She was friendly enough, but a little odd. Never talked to her much. Anyway, I hadn't seen her in a few days, which was strange, so I called in a wellness check. Real sad to hear she was gone...because they will probably turn her house into a rental, which is the worst. Anyway... later, I heard 'bout the other stuff...You never know who you're living next to. My God. Definitely going to make property value go down. Such a shame - on both fronts."

Ms. Petrov had left a note indicating that she had caused the death of Shelley Lazrin, a local woman who has been missing for two months before being found murdered. Evidence found in the basement suggests she had kept Ms. Lazrin captive. A formal autopsy is underway, but it appears she was with child. The cause of death will also be determined during the autopsy but strangulation is suspected.

There was very little linking the two women other than some exchanges on Facebook, in which Ms. Petrov used a false name to communicate with her. However, there has been evidence found in her home that suggests she had a one-sided obsession with the murder victim's husband. Ms. Petrov had several phones which were used to contact Mr. Lazrin anonymously and she had photos of him all over her wall. She kept a journal which documented how she viewed the relationship. However, there is no evidence to support that these encounters ever occurred.

Her former partner, Detective Derzo, has declined to comment. The Belmar Police department also declined to comment.

This story is still developing. Please check back for updates as we uncover more about this bizarre love triangle and the unfortunate loss of two lives.

Five Months after Shelley's death

KYLIE HEARD the door open and shut. She quickly closed her journal and stuffed it under her pillow. "Hey dad!" she yelled as she got up to go meet him. Right away, she noticed the big smile on his face. "I'm guessing work went well?"

"I just got word that we are closing on another house."

Kylie hugged her dad. "Congrats! That's two this month already! Can you pick me up from basketball practice? Molly's mom is going to pick me up soon and we will get dinner before heading to the school."

Lyle nodded in approval. Things were settling into a rhythm, one that wasn't quite right but was manageable. Slowly there were bits of joy and normalcy creeping in and all they could hope was that each day would get easier and easier.

* * *

Excerpt from the personal diary entry of Kylie Lazrin

Today I was getting ready, just doing my makeup and out of nowhere the grief hit me so intensely. My hands started shaking and I dropped the large mirror I was holding. Despite my dad being on a work call, he rushed to my side. We both got on the ground to pick up the pieces.

And there I saw the shattered mirror reflecting our image back to us. It was like my mother was there with me, giving me a message. She whispered, "You may feel like you are in pieces, but you are still fully there within every piece." I whispered back, "Thank you!" And my dad, not privy to this conversation replied, "You're welcome." A sense of peace washed over me and I threw myself into his arms.

I am forever broken, but I am still here.

Dear reader,

You just read an independently published book! How awesome are you! If you enjoyed this book, please spread the word. Tell a friend, suggest it be your book club's next pick, leave a review and post this book on your social media sites.

If you are interested in following my writing journey, including my next book coming Spring 2026, please use the QR code to follow me.

Can't wait to share the next book with you.

Best,

A.L.L.

Blackout Girl

A PSYCHOLOGICAL THRILLER BY AMBER LEIGH LARRAIN

March 2024

"The 'Blackout Girl' is in the interrogation room," a deep voice dripping with disdain said.

I can hear the sound of papers being shuffled and chatter in the distance.

"Pff!" laughed the other officer. "Is that what we are calling her now?"

My mind raced as they continued to talk. All I could hear was mumbling.

I sat at the cold table with my head in my hands, trying to block out as much as I could. The room was mostly empty, aside from three chairs, a table and a recording device in the center. This place was completely sterile—like I was in an insane asylum.

There was nothing in the room to distract me from every fiber of my being trying to scream out that I was not okay—palms sweating, whole body shaking, heart pounding. Nothing about this situation was okay.

A long exhale escaped my mouth. At this point, I was on autopilot, just trying to regulate my body before it became overwhelmed with anxiety. My mind was spinning, and I had no idea why I was here.

I hung on the precipice of going mad. Repeating to myself, *you are okay, you are okay* to keep myself right on the precipice—instead of deep diving off of it.

The two male officers who had been talking about me in the hallway walked in. Their footsteps were heavy, and each step pounded through me as they got closer, making me flinch over and over. Both men pulled out chairs and sat across from me, not taking their eyes off me as they did so.

The first officer was older and you could tell he had been handsome at some point, though age had puffed him out a bit now. The second officer was a young guy who must have been straight out of the police academy. He looked like the type to fly off the handle at any point. If he had been a woman, people would have said he had resting bitch face, but since he's a man, he's just authoritative.

The sternness of their faces unsettled me. I sensed they already had their minds made up about my guilt or innocence. I shifted in my seat trying to get more comfortable; a fruitless task.

Another long, slow exhale. *Keep it together, Isabella. This will all work out.* I kept repeating to myself, though I didn't believe it one bit.

The younger of the officers hit record on the device that sat on the table between us. "State your name for the record," he said with zero emotion in his voice as he stared at me.

"Isabella Frank."

"Today is Friday March 1, 2024. I am Officer Rossi and with me is Officer Clark, with the Hamilton Police Department. Miss Frank, let's start at the beginning. How did you know the victim?"

"What? What victim? Who are you talking about?"

"Don't play stupid with us. Tell us what happened tonight," said the old officer. His pudgy hands resting in his lap.

He was so smug. The way they looked at me, I could feel their distrust before I even opened my mouth. "I told you, I—"

"Blacked out," we all said in unison, their voices tinged with sarcasm.

Biting down on my lower lip, I could taste the tang of blood; metallic and warm. This wasn't going well and I had no idea how to make sense of it. I kept pulling at my sweatshirt as a coping mechanism, unaware of how skittish it made me look. Sure wasn't doing myself any favors.

While thoughts swirled in my head, I paused, trying to think of how to put it all together. I coughed and requested some water. A way to gain a few minutes and hopefully gain a sense of clarity.

The pudgy officer rose to get the water. While he was away, the younger one just glared at me. I had already forgotten both their names as all my mental energy was focused on decoding this situation.

Once I had the water in hand, I took a long swig. Though it only took seconds, time slowed down and it felt like an eternity before I continued.

"I woke up, laying on the ground. No memory of what happened. I was confused because I've never fallen asleep like that before," I lied. "The mental fog—it was like nothing I had ever experienced before. I looked around, trying to figure out where I was, when it was, why I was there. There was an incredible amount of confusion. And then I noticed the blood on the floor. It was everywhere. It was all too much." I gently closed my eyes. I needed a second to pause and regain my composure. "I was convinced that I was in a dream... a nightmare, I mean. Nothing about the situation made sense. I was either imagining it or going crazy."

The two officers side glanced at each other. It was as if they spoke to each other silently, as if they were saying, 'What a load of BS.'

My heart raced even faster. My muscles were stiff as a board.

Realizing this uncomfortable sensation, I recalled what my therapist said and I slowly released the tension muscle by muscle. This only helped relax me a bit. If I couldn't get them to believe me now, I didn't know what I would do.

"You stated you felt like you were going crazy. Do you often feel like you're going crazy? Like you can't control your emotions?" Officer Rossi asked me.

Their accusations caused a lightning bolt of anger to pulse through me. I ran my fingers through my dark brown hair in the hopes of self-soothing, but there was a cold gooey feeling on my fingers as I did so.

"Dammit! I didn't hurt anyone!" I barked as I slammed my hand on the table. When I lifted it, all that hung between us was silence... and the bloody imprint of my palm.

Get your copy to continue Isabella's story...